COLIBRI INVESTIGATIONS
THE STELLAR SNOW JOB

MARIE HOWALT

Denver, Colorado

Published in the United States by:
Spaceboy Books LLC
1627 Vine Street
Denver, CO 80206
www.readspaceboy.com

ISBN: 978-1-951393-14-4
First printed August 2022

Praise for THE STELLAR SNOW JOB

"Marie Howalt's *The Stellar Snow Job* is a wonderful and zany space trip with a universal humane message. Highly recommended for all lovers of fun detective stories, endearing characters, and white fur balls with six legs."

— Seb Doubinsky, author of *Missing Signal*, *The Invisible*, and *Paperclip*

"A standout series-debut filled with excellent characters, a fun plot, and a rich sci-fi setting, *The Stellar Snow Job* is a delight. This science fiction world is thoughtfully constructed and naturally engaging (...) Comparisons could be drawn to *The Hitchhikers Guide To The Galaxy* or *Cowboy Bebop*, but this one is in no way derivative of either (...) Fans looking for a light-hearted space adventure need look no further."

— Steph Huddleston, *Independent Book Review*

"Howalt really shows great depth with *Colibri Investigations: The Stellar Snow Job*. Brand new compelling characters, entirely new worlds, societies, and alien beings flood Howalt's short debut to this exciting new series. By marrying noir and sci-fi, Howalt's canon is impressively expanded and opens the door for many exciting stories to follow."

— William M. Brandon III, author of *Welcome to Spring Street*, *The Exile The Matriarch and The Flood*, and *Silence*

"Original and tongue-in-cheek (...) A rip-roaring space adventure. Howalt's clever latest expertly combines well-executed action with witty banter between authentic characters. (...) the relentless tension, spirited characters, and witty dialogue keep the pages flying. (...) Readers will be delighted to know Richard, Eddie, and Alannah as they are pushed to confront impossible dangers in the lead-up to an exhilarating climax. Fans of intelligent, witty sci-fi will be wowed."

— *The Prairies Book Review*

"I'm a sucker for a fleshed out universe. The less I need to wonder how things work, the less effort is required for me to suspend disbelief. So when Howalt explained in-universe how VoidNet and PlaNet (the intergalactic internet) functioned, I nearly squealed in delight. (...) Let's face it. I was always going to like this book. It ticked all my niche boxes (...) *The Stellar Snow Job* shows Marie Howalt can deliver lovely characters and compelling worlds that jumps out at lightspeed even in smaller dosage."

— Aden Ng, author of *The Chronicles of Tearha* series, and editor at *Ombak Magazine*

"Howalt has a knack for creating complex and instantly likeable characters and knocks it out of the park with Colibri's cast. (...) The writing itself is polished. It pulls you in with its careful pace and style, masterfully interspersed with humour. (...) If you're bored of the same old science fiction and looking for an off the rails space adventure, sensational worldbuilding, fantastic characters, and LGBTQ+ representation, Colibri Investigations: The Stellar Snow Job is the book for you."

— Kathy Joy, author of *Last One to the Bridge*

For my parents who met the *Colibri*'s crew three decades ago
and encouraged me to pursue my passion

Although draevere still largely prefer actual meat from slaughtered animals, most contemporary restaurants catering to the galactic audience have vegetarian and vegan options. So, if you aren't feeling ready to get your proteins the traditional way, there will be plenty of choices to pick from. If you find yourself on Satarim Station in the Kaaloen system, I especially recommend The Green Gothaa which, despite its name, does not actually have gothaa—or any other endangered species—on the menu.

Should you, however, be looking for affordable draever street food or a place to have a drink with the locals of Satarim, there are plenty of smaller establishments to seek out. Please use your patch to scan the code below for an extensive list, and personal suggestions, from yours truly.

— Alannah Jackson, *Dining with Draevere*

1

OPEN MIND, OPEN HEART

"Isn't Motarpria a restricted planet?" Alannah asked, glancing up from the patch display floating ethereally between her hands against the backdrop of her employer's office.

Lisa Boucher tilted her head slightly as if considering this argument. Behind her, the screen taking up most of the wall morphed from a silent clip of space into a gorgeous view of a beach with a single figure surfing the green waves. She was dressed in a grey suit with few embellishments and a lot of business attitude and sharp angles.

Alannah always looked professional for these in-person meetings too, but professional didn't have to mean boring. In fact, it really can't when your profession involves traveling the galaxy and having fun. Today, she had opted for a semi-formal light blue shirt with a floral pattern that only showed when the light hit the fabric just right. It was tucked into a pair of pants—with multiple practical pockets—and cinched at the waist by a broad ecoleather belt. The pockets were key. You never knew when you'd pick up trinkets or snack samples for later inspection.

"That depends on your definition of restricted, doesn't it?" Boucher mused.

"I wouldn't think so," Alannah said. In her experience, things were either legal or they weren't. Every planet or station she visited came with clear instructions for travelers. On some planets, weapons were strictly prohibited to such a degree that you could not bring even a pocket knife. On others, your inventory was inspected upon arrival, and any heavily perfumed products were confiscated and put in sealed bags to be returned only when you left. But numerous planets out there were not cleared for interstellar or interplanetary visitors at all. Motarpria happened to be one of them.

Boucher's smile didn't waver. The clip behind her changed into a view of a lush blue forest. "Motarpria is located in the draevere's Kaaloen system," she said.

Alannah already knew that. Her general astrographical knowledge was pretty good. It was part of her job, after all.

"While it has not officially been cleared for visitors, it is only a matter of time at this point. The native inhabitants are on the verge of space travel. They most likely have already discovered their neighboring planet, and all the activity going on there, including Kaaloen's orbiting space station. It's no longer isolated from the rest of the galaxy. Hasn't been since the draevere settled on Kaaloen. And Starlite Planetary Guides likes to keep one step ahead. We want to be able to publish information for the common people the moment the restrictions are no longer in place. See what I'm getting at?"

Alannah did. It would be a great gig. Imagine writing the first ever travel guide to Motarpria. Imagine publishing the first stills of the flora and fauna of a brand new tourist destination. And to do so even before the wendek, whose efficiency when it came to marketing was always light-years ahead of everyone else...

"Alannah?"

Alannah took a deep breath. She ran a hand through her newly-dyed pastel purple hair as if a decision might spill out of her curls. It didn't. "This ship you are talking about," she began, "does it have the proper clearance for a survey?"

"Of course," Boucher replied airily. "Alannah, you will be the first human being to set foot on this foreign soil! It's an opportunity of a lifetime."

"Why me?" Alannah asked. She wanted to just accept the job, but a small part of her still needed convincing. Starlite

Planetary Guides had so many freelance writers spread all over the galaxy. Some of them a lot more aggressive in their research than she was.

Boucher smiled and leaned across the table, touching Alannah's arm with her pale, manicured fingers for a confidential, reassuring moment. "I want you, Alannah, because you are the best. You connect with the audience in a way that few others can manage. And not only with our human readers. You write with galactic appeal. That's real talent. And I want to give you this opportunity to stand out."

"Thank you." Alannah glanced from Boucher's now retreating hand to the display. It was hard not to get a bit flustered at this praise from a person so high in the hierarchical structure of Starlite. She knew her employer wasn't only doing this to boost Alannah's writerly reputation. She mostly wanted to sell a lot of travel guides. But being handpicked for a job exactly because her work was likely to sell well... That was flattering. Alannah had worked relentlessly, from writing for free for exposure—as if that ever put food on anyone's table— for a small interstellar publication rating restaurants on various planets, to her first job as a junior editor at a local publisher on her home planet, to finally being able to live off her travels and her words... And all that had brought her here.

"I should mention, you will have to sign an NDA along with the rest of the party you will be going with. But in addition to the standard expenses and salary for your work, there's a bonus in it. Since you will be going into... shall we say, *uncharted territory*, we'd like to sweeten the pot? What do you say?" Lisa Boucher's smile was confident and contagious.

It was indeed an opportunity of a lifetime. And Alannah trusted Boucher had the facts right and Motarpria would be cleared for tourism soon. The militant draevere simply wouldn't let them go there otherwise. Things were still a bit touchy between the two species after the skirmishes at the time of humankind's inclusion in the Union. Besides, the result of her trip to Motarpria would not be published before it cleared, and at that point, nobody would know when the trip itself took place. Alannah nodded. "Yes. I'll take it," she said.

"Splendid," Boucher beamed, "I'll send the contract to your patch right away." Her fingers moved rapidly over the display hovering above the patch on her own wrist. A fraction of a second later, a subdued ping told Alannah she had received the document. "I can't wait to read what you come up with. I'm almost jealous of you, to be honest."

A smile spread on Alannah's face. She was getting that giddy feeling in her stomach that she always got at the prospect of something new. This was why she did it. Sure, she liked writing, liked putting her experiences and observations into words. She liked aiming her patch and capturing stills and clips to illustrate her writing. And she liked being a name to be reckoned with in the publishing industry. But what she was in love with were the experiences themselves. The sight of a planet she had never been to before. Talking to all sorts of people from all sorts of species. The culmination of all her preparations, whether they entailed inoculations against foreign diseases, getting used to grav boots with settings tailored for a specific location, or just reading up on social customs. She was in it for the way her job opened her mind and her heart.

And this one would be something entirely new and special. She would be unprepared because she was the first. It was a little daunting. But when had Alannah Jackson ever declined a job because it was daunting? She would nail this one like she did everything else.

"When do I leave?" she asked.

If you are new to interstellar sightseeing, it can be hard to decide where to begin. Are you longing for a hike through the red grasslands of Zemahln? Are you pining to experience the nightlife of Ganmak's cities? Or are the monuments of early draever culture a must-see from your bucket list?

Regardless of your preferences, there is a Starlite Planetary Guide for you. In this volume, we have collected all the general information you need to get started.

Before setting out on an interstellar trip, it is highly recommended to brush up on your Standard. It will be expected that you can communicate smoothly with wendek, draevere, zetois and åayu alike, and the inhabitants of even the most remote settlements have been learning Standard since before humankind even knew the Union existed, as you might be aware.

Nowadays, we have mandatory Standard classes starting in primary school on Earth, as well as at the majority of our settlements and space stations. While many of us still use our native languages among ourselves, especially planet-side, and while preserving our linguistic cultures and diversity is important, so, too, is the ability to communicate smoothly in Standard.

The younger generations living on space stations or recently established settlements often mix English, Chinese, Arabic, Spanish, Hindi, or other Earth native languages with Standard when they speak among themselves. But when it comes to universality, everybody speaks Standard. One might argue that fluency in Standard is not only imperative when communicating with other species, but also offers a huge advantage when interacting with other humans.

If your Standard is rusty, or if you don't feel entirely confident, don't worry. Starlite has put together a guide that will bring you up to speed in no time. Use the code below to connect your patch to our Standard QuickCourse and start learning today.

— Alannah Jackson, *Interstellar Sightseeing 101*

2

WHAT'S YOUR SIN?

"So," the waiter said as he placed the glasses on the table, "how long have you two been together?" He was speaking Standard although humans were currently the only patrons in the half empty bar and he must have heard the two of them arguing in English.

Richard looked up at him, mildly inquisitive and smooth as fuck, in a way that suggested he had understood every word.

Eddie wrinkled her nose in reply and gestured to Richard. "Ew," she said, which was pretty universal when it came to languages.

"Thanks a lot," Richard said in English.

Eddie shrugged and raised her glass, ignoring him for the moment to smile at the waiter. "Thank you," she said in Standard before taking a mouthful of whisky that warmed the back of her mouth and all the way down her throat. Hopefully this would quell certain other urges, at least for a short while.

The waiter lingered by their table. He was curious. And probably bored. "Where are you from?" he asked.

"Córdova," Eddie replied.

By now, Richard's grey eyes had started to ping-pong between them. "Earth," he said which was technically true, although he only lived there for the first few years of his life and to Eddie's knowledge had not been back there for a decade. "Do you want to sit?"

"Really?" the waiter almost gasped. He scanned the surroundings and then quickly slipped into the empty chair at their table. "I'm saving up to go there one day. What's it like?"

Eddie downed the rest of her drink in one gulp. She pushed a strand of hair out of her face. It was just long enough to get in her eyes and, unlike Richard's annoyingly controllable hair, it tended to do exactly that.

Richard arched a perfect eyebrow at her. "Do you want another one?" he asked.

"Nah, it's fine," she said and stood up. "You enjoy yourself. I'll see you back in the chick." Having to listen to her boss humblebrag about his connection to the cradle of humanity, and the waiter being charmed into flirting with the tall, mysterious and handsome captain would not improve her restlessness. She needed to move. Needed something to focus her attention on that was not the private investigator who hadn't been able to find them a job in a subjective eternity. Leaving Richard to take care of the bill was the only fringe benefit left to cash in.

"Don't get into trouble," Richard told her, making it sound like a joke even though they both knew it wasn't.

"Find us a job and I won't, Dick," Eddie retorted. She was already turning away from him, so he probably didn't catch it. She pulled her vintage ecoleather jacket off the back of the chair and shrugged into it on her way out of the establishment.

The jacket wasn't strictly necessary on Kronborg. The space station's climate was intended to match a warm spring day in the northern hemisphere on the planet it orbited. Whether it did, Eddie didn't know. She had only visited the settlement's capital on Bohr during the winter, and she remembered freezing her ass off.

The artificial lighting was reduced to a dim glow overhead, mimicking the daylight cycle and giving the impression of night time in any big city on a human-settled world, or back on Earth.

Eddie shoved her hands into the pockets of her jacket and began to walk. She could take the pipeline from the nearby stop directly to the docks, but... It was too early to head back now.

She and Richard had come to this district to have fun. To see the sights. To hook up with someone, maybe. And definitely not each other like the waiter had suggested. For so many reasons. Oh, but who the hell was she kidding? She'd gone ahead and done all that the first few days they were here. The only reason she had gone with Richard today was to distract herself from the withdrawal symptoms that were starting to creep up on her. How long was it now? Definitely more than a Córdovan week, or one and a half on Earth. She was deliberately not counting the days. But she was beginning to ache for a hit, there was no denying that.

A couple of kids passed her, talking, laughing. What were they? Fifteen? They looked perfectly at home here. Probably had parents who were part of the permanent staff on Kronborg. They might be employed by station control, be teachers, chefs, dock workers, souvenir salespersons, or even officers in the local branch of the Terran Defense Force for all Eddie knew.

On an impulse, Eddie turned away from the main street, away from the signs blinking back and forth between English, Standard, and some Scandinavian language she didn't know. Probably Swedish or whatever was spoken where the station's namesake was located on Earth.

On either side of her, the shops and bars and various lounges were nondescript and free of advertisements. The narrow street was more like an alley, a secret that potential customers might find only with intention or by accident.

As her eyes adjusted to the lowering light, Eddie noticed another person coming toward her. It was a man, probably in his early thirties like her. He struck Eddie as familiar for split a second until she realized it was just the uniform. The midnight blue coveralls of Trans World Trading were, romantically, supposed to symbolize the vast celestial sky that the TWT's ships traversed in order to bring goods from one human settlement to the next, as well as between other stations and planets in the Union. That familiar pilot symbol on the breast pocket caught Eddie's eye, although she could have guessed this guy's profession even without it. The man smiled at her and nodded, and Eddie felt like punching him in the mouth. She didn't punch him in the mouth. Instead, she gave him a quick nod and pretended to check the time on her patch.

For fuck's sake. It had been seventeen Earth months. Seventeen. That she did keep track of, because she was doing fine now. She had a job. She had a ship to fly. It shouldn't feel like a punch in the gut to see a TWT pilot. Involuntarily, her hand moved to the small bump on her arm where the connector was embedded. If only Richard would land them a gig soon. She had had enough of Kronborg.

And here, Eddie realized, was the seedy part of the station. She had stomped along feeling sorry for herself without noticing the slow transformation around her. That was what happened... Yeah, because she hadn't made it here on purpose... Not at all...

A beat echoed from the structures around her, changing in speed and volume as it deflected off the surroundings. A group of maybe 10 people moved to the rhythm, one of them pushing this way and that, dancing, shoving the sound around. Her patch was resting on a barrel, and its display was projected midair, emitting blinking lights that changed in color and intensity every time she moved. She wasn't bad at all. The DJs at the clubs in the area had nothing on her, although her sound was tinnier, and there was no fancy dance floor or attached bar selling expensive drinks. Somehow, it felt more authentic. Like the pulse of the station.

Eddie slowed down, listening to the music, and watching the group. One of them was a draever and another a wendek, both of them tall, but that was about the only similarity between them. The draever was built like a truck and stamped along to the music while looking decidedly aggressive to Eddie's human eyes. The wendek was slight and graceful. Their odor-proof facemask was dangling from a band around their neck, which was probably a compliment to the people around them. The rest of the dancers were humans, like the DJ, and the majority of Kronborg's permanent inhabitants.

A girl with a drink in her hand called out to Eddie; an invitation to join the party. Eddie hesitated, then approached the group. Why not? It wasn't as if she had anything better to do on the station, and she could only do so much in the chick waiting for Richard.

The wendek sized her up in a way that would have come across as suggestive from a human, but Eddie wasn't sure it was intentional. They breathed in, probably assessing the whisky on her breath, or some subtle undertone of her deodorant, or pheromones that she wasn't even aware of. Her nephew could do that, and he was only half wendek.

"Hey!" The dancer who had motioned for Eddie shouted at her over the music, moving rhythmically closer in a way that should have been ridiculous, but was actually kind of sexy.

"Hey," Eddie replied, then gestured toward the DJ. "She's good."

"Yeah," the dancer said, glancing over her shoulder at the DJ who was now performing a series of slow motion movements with one arm while at the same time keeping up the beat with the other hand. "I'm Tam."

"Eddie," Eddie said. She hoped she wasn't expected to dance. There was only one kind of dance she was interested in and excelled at, and it did not involve moving her hips and using her feet. "Where did you get the drink?"

Tam beamed at her in the way only happily drunk people can beam at someone. She took hold of Eddie's hand and pulled her toward a garbage disposal unit next to the makeshift screen the DJ was working. A row of ecoplast cans were lined up, some of them already punctured while others were intact.

"How much?" Eddie asked.

Tam grinned at her and licked her lips and Eddie knew she could get one for free. Tam was drunk enough for that, but Eddie, sadly, wasn't quite there yet. Apparently, Tam realized that too. "10 units," she said and held out a can to Eddie.

Contraband. Probably smuggled in from somewhere. Eddie quickly pulled up the payment tab on her patch and scrolled down the list to find Tam. Since there could not possibly be that many people named Tamara in a radius of a few hundred meters, Eddie transferred the funds without asking if Tamara Jeong was the right one.

"Thanks," Tam said.

Eddie nodded and took the can, pushed her thumb into the perforated area and raised the beer to her lips quickly before it spilled.

"Cheers!" Tam said, holding up her own can.

"Cheers," Eddie replied and drank again. It wasn't good beer, but it would serve the purpose.

The music changed again, to something slower with a steady pulse and an overlay of faster percussion. Eddie, tapping her foot despite her resolve not to dance, looked over her shoulder when she heard someone shouting.

"Now the party can get started for real," Tam said into Eddie's ear. Her breath reeked of beer. Eddie didn't need to be a wendek to discern that.

Eddie watched the newcomer attract a lot of attention from a couple of the other dancers. He put a bag onto one of the garbage disposal units and glanced around as if to make sure no one was looking. At least no one who wasn't supposed to.

"Come on," Tam said, tugging at Eddie.

But before they had even reached the newcomer, Eddie realized what this was all about. He was pulling out a couple of small, transparent vials from the bag, handing them to the dancers around him and getting funds transferred after a quick inspection of the goods.

"One for each of us, Frederik," Tam shouted at the newcomer before Eddie had time to object.

The newcomer, Frederik, smiled at Tam. They knew each other, Eddie gathered. He held up two vials. Light blue fog was curling around in them.

"Thanks, but I'm good," Eddie said, smiling in what she hoped was a way that suggested she was quite sure she didn't want any but perfectly okay with the others taking a breath.

"First one's on me," Tam offered.

"I'm fine. Really. You go ahead," Eddie said.

The dealer's eyes narrowed. "It's harmless," he said.

Tam kept beaming. "It's only mist. You just make a hole in the lid and breathe in."

"I know," Eddie replied. Damn, how she knew. "But no thanks." If someone offered her 10,000 units for free, it would be easier to decline than a vial of mist. Her body and mind were crying out for stimulants. The alcohol helped, but only a bit. Taking a breath with Tam would do wonders. She would feel great, she would fly even without a ship around her, and the urge scratching for attention at her insides would go away. Yeah, she would feel fantastic for a while, and then she would come crashing down, and picking herself up again without help from another vial... and then another... and another... would be too hard. Been there, done that, not a fan.

"Okay, just one for me then," Tam said.

Frederik waited for her to transfer the payment and studied Eddie in the meantime.

And no matter how much she wanted to be okay with it, no matter how hard she wished she could stay and have a good time, Eddie knew she had to leave before she gave in.

"You want something stronger?" the dealer asked.

Eddie almost physically recoiled. "What? Why? No," she said.

Frederik snorted. "Oh, come on. You're practically drooling and you say you don't want mist. What's your sin? Pink? No, let me guess," he added, smirking, "you want a shot of hyper, don't you?"

Hell yes, she wanted a shot of hyper. But she was in control. She would have it as soon as they had a reason to jump and until then, she would stay clean. That was the deal she had struck with Richard, and she was not going to blow that because of this jerk. "No," she said, "I don't."

The dealer raised his eyebrows. He had seen right through her. "I have some. Straight from... Let's just say someone who has access to the good stuff."

"Good for you," Eddie said. "But I'm not interested. That shit is addictive."

"So I hear. Guess you'd know."

"Hey," Tam cut in before Eddie could raise the fist that had involuntarily curled at her side. "Eddie's not crazy, Frederik," she said to the dealer. "And if you really have hyper, you'd better shut up about it." She shrugged at Eddie. "We can do pretty much what we want out here," she said, indicating the vial in her hand, "but no one turns a blind eye when it comes to hyper being used for rec."

"I have to go," Eddie said.

Where had this guy even obtained hyper? Tam was right; it was restricted more than ever now, to be used only by professional pilots, and even for them the regulations were tight. The TWT pilot she had met earlier... Eddie scoffed. It didn't matter one way or the other.

"Stay for another beer," Tam said. "Come on."

"I'm sorry," Eddie said, forcing a smile. "It was fun, but I have to go."

"Come back if you need a shot," Frederik called after her.

Eddie didn't slow down. She was going back to the chick to wait for Richard. Get some sleep maybe. Listen to music loud enough to drown out the teeny tiny voice in the back of her head telling her she should have taken the offer, that she could go back and find the dealer. The chick was an extension of the ship, and it would help remind her why she had to stay clean.

As an alternative to booking your journey on a regular raphinae or laridae class cruiser or passenger ship, you might want to consider checking your local PlaNet for private vessels to plan your budget holiday. Lots of smaller passer class ships advertise their travel plans well in advance and offer a cabin to civilian startrotters.

Traveling on a smaller ship may not provide you with the luxurious accommodations of some cruisers, but it sports the same artificial gravity system, and the same thick pelso plating on the outer hull to keep you and the crew safe, sparing you the hassles and hazards of zero G.

Going from your local station to the ship in question is, as with the bigger classes of ship, done by chick. If you are new to spaceship lingo, please let me assure you that there isn't some kind of misogynist joke in the name. Spaceship personnel call shuttlecraft "chicks" in reference to juvenile birds because all human ship classes have long been named after bird families.

On any smaller ship, you will often have to dine in the crew's galley, and you might even share quarters. And keep in mind that these trips may require several hyperspace jumps, or even make some journeys the slower, sometimes grittier, good, old-fashioned way. But take it from someone who has been a professional tourist for the past five years—It can be a great experience to huddle up with, and listen to the stories of the people who, when you think about it, make the whole thing possible.

— Alannah Jackson, *The Galaxy on a Budget*

3
THE COLIBRI

The docks were as quiet as they ever got. It was four in the morning and everybody with a regular day job was asleep. Richard Hart did not have a regular day job. He never did. Before starting up his own investigations business, he was an intelligence officer in the Terran Defense Force. And even on simple missions, regular, daily routines were mythical creatures.

Richard squinted at the glowing signs above each of the jetties. Hell if he could remember where they had parked. That was what he paid Eddie for. Well, that and taking him across vast distances in space so he could do his job. Okay, and sparring with him quite often because two minds were better than one.

Somewhere to his right, a chick took off, gliding purposefully through the labyrinth of transparent walls that led to the airlocks and onward to the outer docking ring. That's also where Richard was going. If he could find his chick and his pilot. Stopping, he ran a hand through his hair and scanned the row of jetties. There. Finally. The chick was parked almost right in front of him. He hoped Eddie wasn't looking out at him.

A quick retina scan, and the door slid open. The lights didn't come on when Richard stepped inside, a clear sign that Eddie was here and had told them not to. A faint smell of beer and sweat met his nostrils. It wasn't much different from the stench lingering on his clothes. Were it not for the fabric's stain absorbing qualities, Richard would have boasted quite a spatter discoloring the sleeve of his grey shirt. That drunk, clumsy draever spilled her drink all over the place.

Eddie was curled up in the pilot's seat with her jacket draped over her, the lights from outside reflecting off the ecoleather. The part of her dark brown hair that she let grow out more than a single centimeter was messily tousled. Somehow, she looked more peaceful than Richard had seen her in days. He knew that would only last until she woke up and fixed her intense, brown eyes on him, demanding to know if it was time to go yet.

Richard eased himself into the seat next to her. Should he try to get some sleep here or just wake her up? His normal impulse would be to poke her, but she was on edge these days. He wanted a job as much as she did, but her restlessness one-upped his financial worries and mounting boredom.

Eddie muttered something Richard couldn't possibly make out in the darkness.

"So, you're awake," he replied.

Something else he couldn't understand. Either she was really drunk or too tired to think, or else she was punishing him for something. "Eddie," he sighed.

Another short string of words—she was awake—and the lights slowly illuminated the cockpit. "Did I wake you up?" Richard asked, now that he could see enough to have an actual conversation with her.

"It's fine," she replied, pushing herself into a sitting position, unfolding her legs and stretching.

Richard studied her. "You look like hell," he said.

Eddie rolled her eyes. "Wow, thanks."

He shrugged. It was true. She looked like she hadn't slept for days. She didn't look as rough in the bar earlier. "Something happen?"

"No," she said. "Want to go back to the ship?"

Richard nodded. He wasn't going to press her for answers. What did he know about hyper withdrawal, anyway? At least she seemed fairly sober and not high on something else. "I thought we should catch a few hours of sleep. And," he added, "if nothing's come our way in the morning, we'll go somewhere else."

Eddie fixed him with a sharp look.

"It's odd that we haven't had any incoming jobs for a while," he continued, making up the reason as he went along. "Maybe people are only looking for someone exclusively on their own PlaNet." It was true, technically, that some potential clients may use local means only, but the majority would search for a private investigator on VoidNet databases as well. Especially if their concern was interstellar. Richard knew Eddie could tell he was making the call for her benefit, but she didn't argue. "You good to fly?"

"Buckle up," Eddie replied and tossed her jacket aside. Sturdy restraints slid around them as Eddie began to back them out of the booth, away from the jetty and into the transparent maze.

Richard sat back and let her do the work. He could fly a chick, but Eddie was obviously much more qualified at steering anything in three-dimensional space than he would ever be. He was a good driver when it came to cars, but the difference between controlling a vehicle bound to a landmass and a craft capable of moving between planets and stars was as big as the difference between riding a bicycle and driving a truck.

He brought up his patch and swiped through the tabs he'd left open. "What do you know, a wealthy miner on Johnson has died and left me his fortune," he snorted.

Eddie turned. "And all they need is your account information?"

"Apparently. I'll be rolling in units," he said and deleted the message after, uselessly, blocking the sender. If they didn't get a job soon, maybe they would begin a scamming career. They could hardly do worse than some of the idiots in the game now.

He swiped and refreshed his search. No luck on the virtual PlaNet signpost of Kronborg either.

It wasn't the first time he'd gone without a job for a while, but Richard hated it. He didn't leave the military to sit around in a space station doing nothing. All right, so he didn't exactly leave the military. He'd been medically discharged, and there was no choice there. If it had just been an acute illness, the Terran Defense Force might have kept him on. But auditory verbal agnosia with no cure in sight on top of that? To the Force, working around that inconvenience was simply too long and too complicated a process. Try being the one who has to deal with it every single day. Fighting his way back to health and a somewhat normal life and learning how to communicate with other people without relying on his hearing had occupied the first year before he decided to start up his own show.

"What?" he asked, realizing that Eddie had spoken.

"Did you have a good time?" she repeated.

"Yeah, it was all right," Richard replied. "You?"

Her reply was non-verbal, a shrug and a shake of her head so slight that she was probably not aware of it.

Richard didn't press the subject. To tell the truth, he hadn't particularly enjoyed himself either. The first five times he'd tried out Kronborg's nightlife had been great, but after that, it just felt like he was going through the motions.

Here they were, two rejects from their respective career paths, spending their nights drinking and idling time away, pretending they were having as much fun as teenagers out partying for the first time. Richard didn't need the grey hairs at his temples to tell him he was too old for partying several nights in a row.

The first airlock slid open, and Eddie went through. When the outer one opened after a moment, they glided smoothly out into the void. Ships in all sizes, ranging from craft with little room for passengers or cargo to vessels the size of small towns, hung suspended in the vacuum of space in the docking area. None of these were meant to ever touch a planet. They had been built in space and relied on chicks or space elevators to ferry people and objects back and forth.

The *Colibri* was a passer class ship, small by definition. She had room for a crew of five, but one person could fly her, so she was ideal for Richard and Eddie who valued their privacy as much as each other's company. Someone once told Richard you only really got to know someone when you moved in with them. Well, try being cooped up in a spaceship together. It was probably a good thing that he was only slightly less against hooking up with Eddie than she was with him.

Named after a tiny bird native to Earth, the *Colibri* was a fairly sleek little ship—a design left over from a time when spacecraft took off from the planet and had to struggle against atmosphere and gravity.

The only thing that stood out in the *Colibri*'s construction was the broad, hollow belt popping out from her midsection. A core of ridiculous mass density inside the belt spun around the ship as a vital part of the artificial gravity system.

The *Colibri*'s cockpit was at the front, a touch Richard liked for its nod to old fashioned military plane design where the pilot would need to actually look out of the window. As it were, Eddie relied on her sight and her inhumanly quick processing of what she saw, but there was no windshield to look through. No transparent material was dense enough to keep out the background radiation of the universe, so the entire outer hull was covered by pelso plating. Instead, screens mounted inside the cockpit gave the impression that one was looking through a window to space.

The nest was located at the rear of the ship. Eddie guided them along the outside of the hull. The chick turned, and as it approached the nest, its outer doors slid open. In space, the chick's collapsible wings served no purpose, tucking nicely into its tiny frame and ensuring there was plenty of room for it in the nest.

Once inside, the chick glided to a smooth halt. They waited for the outer doors to close, then for the nest to re-pressurize. A green glow lit up the panels all around the edge of the chick when it was safe to get out.

Richard stepped out and took a deep breath of the familiar, dry, recycled air of the *Colibri*. No matter how good the air recycling and purification systems were, the air inside ships and most space stations always had a bit of an artificial, stale tinge to it. With the exception of wendek vessels, of course. They had made air quality an artform.

Eddie patted the side of the chick, and for a moment, Richard was reminded of grainy clips of centuries past where riders would pat their horse after dismounting. At least she didn't have to feed the chick. It automatically sucked up energy from the receptors in the floor.

"Good night," Eddie said.

"Sleep well," Richard replied and looked after her as she retreated down the corridor in the direction of her cabin. Her posture seemed almost normal, her gait as brisk and decisive as usual, but somehow she was a little too purposeful. As if keeping herself on a short leash.

Richard went the other way. A handrail flanked the corridor on one side— a safety precaution in case the artificial gravity failed. Right now, the *Colibri*'s interior was sporting a comfortable 0.9 G. It was close to Earth's gravity, but with the added bonus that things broke less if you dropped them. It also made running a little more fun.

Richard's cabin had just enough room for everything he needed. It had what looked like a large window. In reality, that too was a screen, but it displayed the view from a camera on the outside, so the effect was nearly the same. Instead of curtains, though, the screen had options for dimming the brilliance, changing the scenery displayed to the feed from another camera or a pre-programmed array of clips. He could also just turn it off altogether. Richard rarely changed anything about it. He liked the view.

It was too late for a shower, Richard decided as he undressed. He wanted to get a few hours of sleep as soon as possible so he could get up in the morning, or before noon at least, and magically pull a job out of a black hole to make Eddie happy.

"Lights off," he said.

The *Colibri*'s computer gradually turned down the lights. She never spoke to him. He had disabled that feature as one of the first things after buying her. If the ship needed to give him a message, it would arrive instantly and in writing on his patch. Eddie was subjected to the same treatment unless she was wearing her headset.

Richard pulled the blanket over himself and yawned. He lay looking out at the lights from Kronborg until he fell asleep.

After the development of the hyperdrive—the solution to the unpredictable nature of faster than light travel—and our introduction to the Union (with inclusion in Category 3 under the interstellar laws that we all abide by now), humanity began to settle on other planets, starting with Johnson, and shortly thereafter, Zhao.

As you may know, the third planet humanity settled, Hawking, is the fourth planet from its local star. It is nine tenths the size of Earth and has an atmosphere composed of nearly the exact same components and values. Its gravity is a mere 0.04 percent higher, and the day-night cycle just an Earth hour shorter—remarkably close to what the first humans settling there were used to.

Like all other settled or inhabited planets, Hawking has an orbiting space station: Stonehenge. This is the connection between the planet and the vast space beyond, but it is much more than that. Stonehenge is a city in its own right with schools, law enforcement, and places for religious worship for many denominations. There are also museums, restaurants, recreational parks and a practical pipeline system that will get you from one part of the station to another in no time.

If you are wondering where to get the best black brew on Stonehenge Station, or which spot on Hawking makes the most romantic place to propose to your beloved, this guide has got you covered.

- Alannah Jackson, *Interstellar Sightseeing 101*

4

BECOMING A GOD

"Good morning!" Richard called out as brightly as the flash of the most energetic supernova ever. Eddie was nursing her second cup of black brew in the galley.

When humans began to establish settlements on other planets, coffee had been a stable export. But over time, local substitutes had been made, some synthetic approximations of coffee, and others were brews made from plants that were somewhat similar to coffee beans. All of it was lumped together under the umbrella term *black brew* which meant "as close as we could get to actual coffee" and that you'd never quite know what you were going to get. And as such, coffee was still a valuable export item. Eddie had flown enough cargoes in her former career as a TWT pilot loaded up with the best black brew that humanity could produce, and genuine coffee—rare as it was—was always guarded under lock and key.

She waited to reply until Richard had retrieved his mug of black brew, along with the protein and vitamin rich cereal he pretended to enjoy. He seated himself in the chair on the opposite side of the table, folding his long limbs a bit awkwardly. The problem wasn't as much the size of the galley as the fact that most furniture was bolted to the floor on a spaceship.

"Morning," Eddie said. "You clearly slept well."

He smirked. "Perhaps, but there is a different reason for my exuberance."

"Exuberance, really?" Eddie said. "We're not playing Wordcrawler."

"Mock me all you want," he retorted and swiped at his patch. "I'll just send you the coordinates for our next destination."

A soft ping told Eddie a message arrived. She didn't look down right away. "Destination?" she echoed, hoping it meant what it sounded like it meant.

"Yes. I am meeting a potential... client on Stonehenge Station," Richard said, taking a mouthful of FiberFlakes that he munched with, probably, feigned delight.

Eddie narrowed her eyes. "I'm sorry, I couldn't quite tell if that's client with a capital C or client in quotation marks." There definitely had been a strange, little pause before the word.

Richard took an annoying, stalling sip of his black brew. "I can't tell you much yet."

"There is a client, right?" Eddie asked.

"Yes, there's a client. Their message came through to this system an hour ago," Richard confirmed without hesitation. That much was good, at least. "But they are a Terran Defense Force intelligence officer, and they did not specify anything."

"Old colleague?" Eddie fished. "Come on, you gotta give me something."

"I have met them, but it's been a while. We never worked together professionally before," Richard said. "Look, I will tell you more after the meeting. Do you want to jump or not?"

Eddie crumpled up one of the instant black brew sachets into a tight ball and flicked it at his face. He caught it without missing a beat. "Don't be a dick, Dick," she said. "When are we going?"

"Later today. Unless," Richard added, tossing the sachet from hand to hand and barely concealing a grin, "you'd rather stay here a bit longer."

Eddie rolled her eyes. "I'll get right on it."

"But first," Richard said, "I'd like to finish my breakfast."

"I'll go and get ready to take her out," Eddie replied, swallowed the rest of her black brew and stood up.

"Did you have breakfast?" Richard asked.

None of his business. And Eddie could eat while he was meeting with the client. But in order not to give her boss an excuse to bitch at her, she grabbed her own box of cereal, Crunchy Asteroids, and stuffed a fistful of the multicolored chunks into her mouth. She turned briefly to Richard and nodded emphatically before heading out of the galley.

Eddie wasn't only excited to get away from Kronborg. It was as good or bad as any other space station. She was excited to get jumping. No, not excited. It was a deeper craving deep down in her insides. She needed it. But first, she had to get to the cockpit and get them in position to jump.

Richard had no reason to be in the cockpit with her for that. He didn't really have a reason to be there when she jumped, either, but he preferred to be able to see what was going on. And since he paid her for flying, who was she to argue?

Eddie reached the cockpit, unlocked the safe under the co-pilot's seat and took out a small cylinder. "Hello," she murmured and exhaled. She'd been holding her breath. Which was silly because she knew a handful of doses were left in the safe. She counted them every damn time.

She slipped into her seat, loaded the cylinder so it was ready when she needed it, and put on her headset. "Station control, this is *Colibri* 7346 requesting departure to Stonehenge Station," she said.

She was on hold for a few seconds. Then a voice replied, "This is station control. Please wait for route five to clear, *Colibri*. We will send you the go-ahead signal."

"Thank you. *Colibri* awaiting your go-ahead." Eddie spent the time pulling out the rolled-up tube from the machine she had placed the cylinder in. Her hands were shaking ever so slightly. She clenched, then unclenched them. She had waited for so long. A few more minutes made no difference.

"*Colibri* 7346, this is station control. You are clear to depart via route five. I am sending you the jump coordinates," said the voice in her headset. "Have a nice day."

"Thank you, station control," Eddie replied. A light on the panel in front of her changed from red to green. She touched it and fired up the ship's thrusters. There was a slight vibration for a moment, going from fast to faster, and then becoming an almost unnoticeable hum as Eddie began to steer the *Colibri* out of the station's docking area.

She flicked a glance at the coordinates that would take them to a spot near Stonehenge Station. Obviously, she could jump from any point in space to any other point, and the chances of crashing into another ship when emerging from hyperspace were slim, what with space being fucking huge and ships comparatively teeny tiny. But if you needed to go near any kind of busy hub you stuck to the coordinates you were given. Courier ships and buoys constantly ping-ponged information on which approach route was occupied when, so it was the safest way to avoid accidents. Humanity had learned that the hard way, just like it did most things.

Richard appeared next to Eddie. He slipped into the co-pilot's seat and leaned back to enjoy the view. In the beginning, his insistence on being in the cockpit had annoyed her. An actual co-pilot she would not have minded, but for someone who was not a hyperspace pilot to be there had felt like an odd breach of some privacy she didn't know she needed. She had never explained any of this to Richard, and he had never asked. Instead, he had learned to shut up and only offer assistance if she actually asked for it. And she had learned to accept his presence. It wasn't like she noticed him while she was going through hyperspace. Perhaps it was exactly that lack of awareness that made it so strange.

They cleared Kronborg's docks, and Eddie checked the coordinates and the controls one last time. And then she finally, finally activated the system that injected the contents of the cylinder into her arm.

The problem with lightspeed wasn't so much building the drive. It wasn't about creating a spaceship hull or keeping the interior of the craft habitable for humans. It was about the pilot.

Sure, it was easy enough to push the button and send the ship into hyperspace. Anyone could do that. It was every bit as simple to switch off the hyperdrive as well. Using a detailed map of the space the ship traversed, automatic systems could technically steer the craft around known obstacles. But the thing about hyperspace was that it did not act like normal, predictable three-dimensional space. It was anyone's guess why punching a small hole in the fabric of the universe made normal laws of physics flip a middle finger at automated systems. In that little pocket of another dimension, you found the phenomenon pilots referred to as hyperwind. It wasn't wind like you'd experience it on a planet with an atmosphere; just an unpredictable disturbance that could potentially push you out in the wrong place. There were theories, of course, but Eddie didn't really give a fuck about those. Probably, the phenomenon had to do with chaos theory, which was blamed for everything that made no sense. The point was that a biological entity had to be part of the equation to make it a safe trip unless you opted for a stable wormhole, and that was a whole other can of worms, pun intended. But no human was naturally fast enough to take a ship through hyperspace, so it was a good thing that the human brain had a whole lot of unused potential waiting to be drafted into action.

When Eddie made the jump, she was no longer human. She was a god. The moment the needle pushed a dose of hyper into the connector and it spread like wildfire through her veins and lit up parts of her brain that were never usually active, everything around her slowed to a grinding halt. She could not have a conversation with mere mortals. She became the ship.

She suppressed a sigh of relief as she felt the drug rush to her head. Explaining to someone what hyper was like was impossible. It was not a recreational drug. It wasn't a mellow substance like mist or the kind that made you dance all night long like whatever some wendek kids would breathe for fun. It was better than being drunk. It was better than sex. It transformed you temporarily into a superhuman being.

Eddie jumped.

The *Colibri* broke the barrier of light, folded space like a blanket and shot toward the Hawking system, light years away from Kronborg. Eddie could easily make it in one jump. It was only a couple of hours in normal, objective time. Though she experienced that period quite differently from the person in the co-pilot seat.

She watched solar system after solar system go by, checking the course, checking the computer's calculations, correcting the trajectory when hyperwind pushed her a bit off course, checking the distance to every major body of gravity they passed to make sure they weren't pulled in. She rode on another wave of hyperwind like a surfer on the ocean, cruising for a little while before its direction changed and she had to let it go and chase another wave toward her own goal. She ran the numbers and made sure the *Colibri* was aimed at the exact spot that station control on Kronborg had assigned to her.

Finally, the trip was at its end. Eddie hit the brakes. Not actual brakes. It was a matter of switching off the hyperdrive by the merest movement of her hand.

Space unfolded itself outside the *Colibri*, a rippling kind of sensation that could be felt throughout the ship. She was gliding through normal space, coming up on Hawking, backlit by the local star from this angle. Stonehenge Station was in geosynchronous orbit around the planet and was just rolling into view.

Eddie leaned back in her seat and closed her eyes. The drug was still coursing through her veins. Everything would feel slow and odd for the next hour and then gradually subside into normal, boring, human sluggishness, but even so, she was calm now. She felt better than she had for a week.

Richard coughed, breaking the spell.

Eddie opened her eyes and looked at him. He was getting out of the co-pilot's seat, rolling his shoulders. In comical slow-motion. To him, the whole trip would have been a blur. He turned to her.

"Welcome to the Hawking system," Eddie said. Slowly. Human speed.

"Thank you," Richard replied. "Smooth ride?"

"Smooth ride," she confirmed.

He studied her for a moment, then nodded. "All right. Take her the rest of the way to Stonehenge and let me know when we're ready to dock," he said.

"Of course." She smiled to herself. Richard didn't know what it was like. Couldn't understand. But he knew enough to give her a little while alone to come down again. She told the *Colibri* to approach Stonehenge Station at a leisurely speed and sat back to enjoy the slow ride.

As a second-generation Córdovan, Eddie found it hard to imagine humanity confined to one solar system as it had been before settling on other planets. Even so, humanity was still reeling from the impact of learning it was not alone and that the universe was not as humancentric as sci-fi shows had historically imagined. There was no Federation or Empire led by humans. They were just another species to join the Union, just another species to be told to learn Standard, to adapt to the rules and regulations, to rename the stars on their galactic maps so they corresponded with the names given to them by the peoples living on planets in orbit around them.

Eddie was perfectly okay with it. There was a kind of poetic justice, especially to the white man whose self-proclaimed burden had been lifted from his shoulders and thrust in his face. Some handled it better than others.

At this particular moment, the white man Eddie had just hauled through the galaxy was probably busy changing into a meet-and-greet the client outfit. Usually, that included a jacket with a standing collar and asymmetric closing and a suggestion of lines along the edges. It gave people subtle military associations which made them think of reliability and seriousness. Eddie was pretty sure he would deny any such thing, but she knew it was the case. He wasn't the kind of person who wore much makeup if any, but he could pull it off with his fashionable scruffiness and annoying cheekbones.

Eddie opted out of makeup most of the time and could get away with it perfectly well too. But she prided herself in not giving two units about clients' subconscious associations. She didn't particularly care if anyone thought she looked trustworthy and ambitious or not. She was there to do a job, that was all.

"Stonehenge, this is *Colibri* 7346," she hailed the station as she approached it. "We request docking."

"Hello, *Colibri* 7346. Welcome to Stonehenge Station," a slightly artificial, very British voice replied. "If you are a Trans World Trading transport requesting to dock, please wait for the next available assistant. If you are from the Terran Defense Force, please contact our military docking area by selecting TDF in the menu on your display. If you are a courier vessel, please select CV in the menu on your display. If you are a private vessel, please contact our private docking area by selecting PV in the menu on your display. For other inquiries, please select OI in the menu on your display. If you wish to hear your choices again, please select A in the menu on your display. If you would like to hear this message in Standard, please select S in the menu on your display."

Eddie selected PV. Richard's occupation had 'private' as the first word, after all.

"A docking assistant will be with you shortly. Please wait," the voice said. And then the music began.

"I'm not here to listen to your shitty music," Eddie muttered. Stonehenge Station was always a little more busy than its designers intended. Originally an Earth settlement consisting of a majority of British, Scottish, and Irish citizens, Hawking and its orbiting station had become a hub of mining activity because of the resources in the local asteroid belt between it and the fifth planet in the system.

"This is Stonehenge station control. Thank you for your patience, *Colibrí 7346*. What can I do for you today?" a crisp voice cut through her thoughts.

Eddie wondered if anyone ever wanted something besides docking. "Hello, station control," she replied, "We request permission to dock."

When you travel off-world, you are likely to spot at least one ship from the Terran Defense Force close to every major space station. Despite its archaic name, the TDF doesn't merely take care of the interests of Earth, but of all humans.

The TDF is a branch of the military, but they are largely a peace-keeping institution. On the few occasions they have to show their teeth, it is to keep citizens safe from riots and civil wars. I'm sure we all remember how relatively peacefully the crisis on Johnson was resolved a few years back. During the skirmishes between the draevere and humans, the TDF has also shown proper restraint and willingness to stand down.

I am not telling you this as an act of military propaganda, far from it, but not everybody is used to a visible military presence on their home planet. I have seen tourists blanch at the sight of accipitriformes and strigiformes class ships looming outside space stations and would like to stress the point that the vessels and their crews are not a sign of imminent war, military coups, or anything as sinister as that.

Furthermore, should you find yourself in trouble in your travels to planets and stations of other species, you will usually contact the local authorities first, but in addition to them, you can always get in touch with the human embassy for legal advice and protection. The embassy staff always includes a member of the TDF who will also assist you if the need arises.

- Alannah Jackson, *Interstellar Sightseeing 101*

5
A HUMAN PROBLEM

"Tea?" the adjutant asked Richard. He had already placed a handleless cup on a small, flat saucer on the desk in front of Colonel Micah Dietrich and was pouring the liquid into it.

Richard could count on the fingers on one hand how many times he had been offered tea and not black brew when meeting a client. But Stonehenge was a station founded by the British, and Richard supposed Dietrich embraced the local customs. The scent of the tea, however, was not culturally traditional. Richard was quite sure this was herbal. Possibly green tea? "Yes, please," he said.

The adjutant said something else, but his side was turned to Richard now. It probably had to do with whether he wanted sweetener added, so Richard simply said, "That's fine." He didn't have much of a preference either way when it came to tea.

The adjutant glanced at him in a way that suggested the reply made sense, but had sounded a bit off somehow. Still, he placed a cup in front of Richard too and poured. The aromatic steam twirled upward from the translucent, greenish liquid. Richard wondered if the tea leaves were locally grown or imported from Earth.

"Thank you, Lieutenant Nakano," the Colonel said. "You may leave us." Placing one hand under the cup and the other around it, they raised it to their lips and sipped.

Richard followed suit. Definitely green tea. It didn't have the bitter tang that some other variants had. He studied his potential client over the cup. Micah Dietrich was, if possible, even more strikingly good-looking than the last time Richard saw them. And the Colonel seemed calm and perfectly at ease in the black and silver uniform of the Terran Defense Force.

"How are you, Captain Hart?" Colonel Dietrich asked, articulating each word carefully, but stopping short of the really annoying kind of exaggeration and embarrassing theatrics that most people who were aware of Richard's situation employed when talking to him in person for the first time.

"Quite well," Richard replied, wondering if the Colonel meant Captain as in his previous military rank or as in someone with a ship and a crew, albeit an extremely small crew in his case. "And yourself, Colonel Dietrich? It has been a while."

Once upon a time, they had both been stationed on the planet Zhao, back when Richard was a lieutenant. Dietrich, through some highly classified heroic deed on Earth that Richard did not have the clearance to know any details about at the time, had already earned their captaincy. They were both in intelligence and had gone out for drinks with a handful of other officers once or twice. On one of these occasions, the two of them had been involved in a bit of a scuffle in a bar, but that was the extent of their relationship. Now Richard was a private investigator, and Dietrich, apparently, was the head of military security on Stonehenge.

"Too long," the Colonel said with a genuine smile. "I am happy you could find time in your schedule to pay a visit to your old Colonel."

Micah Dietrich's long and shockingly non-regulation hair was white, but it was definitely not valid as an indication of their age. Richard was fairly certain they were at least a couple of years his junior.

They also had never been his Colonel. Richard Hart had served under several officers during his time in the Force, but Dietrich was not one of them. However, Richard had been summoned to their office on Stonehenge Station via an encrypted message that was very careful not to spill too much information, even to its recipient. So if this was the pretense they were going to go with, Richard was happy to play along.

He didn't have keep it up for long, though. He was answering with a non-specific lamentation on his failure to keep up with the Force when the Colonel made a complicated series of motions on their patch. A code of some kind, Richard assumed.

"Thank you for coming," they continued in a more brisk and less sociable tone. "We can speak freely now."

So whatever they had asked Richard to Stonehenge for, it was so covert that even their adjutant could not be permitted to stay, and they had to scramble the surveillance in their own office. Interesting.

"I am looking to contract you," Dietrich continued, "because I need someone to take care of a delicate matter."

"So I gathered," Richard said, a bit impertinently maybe, but he was not the Colonel's subordinate. His discharge from the military had to come with some perks.

"Are you familiar with the Kaaloen system?" the Colonel asked, pulling up a star chart between the display rods on the desk.

Richard looked at it, then back up at the Colonel's face. "It's under draever jurisdiction." Why, in other words, would the Force covertly contact him about a decidedly non-human solar system?

"Yes," Dietrich agreed. "They settled on the third planet a few of our centuries ago. It was, of course, unpopulated, and they did some planetforming to tailor it to their needs. However, the fourth planet in the system is not uninhabited." They indicated the planet in question with their index finger, and it lit up with information in minuscule writing that Richard was too busy lipreading to delve into. "According to the draevere, the lifeforms there are sentient, but not yet technologically advanced."

"I see," Richard said. But, again, what exactly did that have to do with the Force and, specifically, with him?

"Obviously, the draevere do not venture to that planet. At some point, the lifeforms on it will probably invent a telescope that can detect interplanetary activity and system surveillance, and then steps will have to be taken. Thankfully, that is not our problem to sort out. What is our problem, however," they added with a sigh, "is that a few human ships have gone to the system seemingly with no particular purpose, allegedly to visit Kaaloen or its orbiting station, Satarim. But it has come to our attention that there are almost no records of the crews' activities at all when they leave the system again a few days later. We can track one expensive purchase in an antiques shop at the most. No other credit charges on their patches, no activity on the local PlaNet. Nothing that indicates they do anything at all. It also appears that the ships have a connection with a travel agency, which makes the lack of recorded activity even more suspicious." Dietrich shook their head. They looked like a person who would very much like to get to the bottom of this and preferably taking care of it, themself. Richard knew the type. He happened to be it.

"That is a human problem," Richard agreed. "But why..." He made a vague gesture. Why not one of the Colonel's own people?

Dietrich steepled their fingers in front of them and looked at him over their hands. They said something.

And this was not an unimportant tea preference situation. So as much as he hated pointing to his disadvantage, Richard put a polite smile on his face. "I'm sorry. I didn't quite catch that, Colonel."

The Colonel blinked. It was amazing how quickly people slipped into their various habits after only a few minutes of conversation. Dietrich was even a high ranking intelligence officer for crying out loud. You'd almost think they did it on purpose. "Oh, I do apologize," they said. They had the decency to look suitably embarrassed.

Richard shook his head. "Please go on."

"It is indeed a human problem, but it is also a very delicate one. And it is my particular problem because the travel agency funding the activity is located here on Stonehenge. I believe the suspects somehow circumvent draever station security and leave orbit by chick. But I have no hard evidence that they are going to the fourth planet. And I do not want to attract attention to this by going to Satarim Station in any official capacity, especially not to ask the draevere to look into the matter because of our... shall we say fragile relationship? Besides, I would have to verify human presence on the restricted planet, which in itself is a breach of interstellar regulations. So I need someone competent and with experience in military intelligence who is not directly affiliated with the Force."

"Ah. You need someone to take the fall if things go down the proverbial black hole," Richard summarized.

Dietrich's left eyebrow twitched, but they quickly smoothed their face back into a neutral expression. "I would not put it quite like that."

Richard was rather curious as to how they would to put it, then, but he wasn't here to discuss semantics. "Do I have the authority to apprehend the suspects on the restricted planet or only confirm their presence?" he asked.

"If it can be done without alerting the native population or the draevere to your presence, apprehension and retrieval will be preferable," the Colonel said. "If there are too many individuals or other circumstances making it unsafe, confirmation will do. Energy signatures, stills, clips, anything you can get back to me."

Richard nodded. "Do we know how the suspects manage to get away from the station without causing any suspicion from the draevere? And how about their schedule?"

"The schedule is the simplest part," Dietrich said. "We are keeping an eye on human ships docking at Satarim Station. If the past conduct is anything to go by, a ship should arrive in between 12 and 72 Earth hours. As for how... The draevere have surveillance throughout the system, but we believe the suspects have a contact on Satarim who helps them get clear of the station without attracting any attention. It is likely a draever employed by station control, which is another reason why the Force can't ask too many questions without arousing suspicion." Dietrich looked almost peevish now. Oh yes, they would definitely prefer to be part of the action themself. "Well, once the suspects are far enough away, it should be possible to go under the radar if they are doing it by chick. It wouldn't raise any red flags in the way that a ship would. I will hand over the relevant leads for you to follow up on if you take the job."

Richard nodded. It sounded like an almost radiation proof scheme, he had to give the suspects that.

"And," the Colonel added, slowly, "in the interest of complete transparency, if you are discovered on or en route to or from the fourth planet, especially if your quarry turns out not to be there, the Force may find itself with no other choice than to deny any involvement."

Richard took a long sip of his herbal tea. It didn't hurt to let the Colonel stew for a little bit. To think about it before he made up his mind. He put down the cup and pulled up a display on his patch at an angle that Dietrich would not be able to see. "Excuse me," he said. He didn't know how long he would need to stay in the Kaaloen system, or exactly what equipment he would need. But he could run the numbers for the ship's and the chick's energy cost, take Eddie's dosages of hyper into consideration and add the fee he usually charged per day. Plus a handsome bonus for the risk involved. "I assume you don't want me to send you my approximation of the charges or a standard contract?"

The Colonel waved their hand dismissively. "No. You can tell me."

Richard did.

To their credit, Dietrich did not try to haggle. "That is fine. In the light of the sensitive nature of this job, I hope you don't mind a physical contract."

"It's been a while since I've seen one of those," Richard replied, smiling, "But by all means." The only paper he ever saw was in books that, for one reason or another, the owner had opted to buy the physical edition. While accumulation of analog objects was trendy now and then, it was not a particularly practical hobby to entertain on a small spaceship.

"Good. Let us settle it right away," Dietrich said and pulled open a desk drawer. They retrieved a few sheets of paper, an actual fountain pen, and a folder. Richard wondered if this equipment was an affectation of Dietrich's, a nostalgic preference in writing utensils, or if they only kept the paraphernalia for exactly these kinds of contracts. The Colonel handed the folder to Richard. "This is the full mission briefing. Perhaps you would like to acquaint yourself with it while I draft the paperwork."

Normally, Richard was the one who made contracts for his clients to sign and not the other way around. But this wasn't the usual cheating spouse or lost pet case. He opened the folder and was met with a few pages that were clearly printouts of digital files. There was something awkward about the flattened version of the 3D image of the ship model they were looking for. Richard barely stopped himself before he attempted to rotate the picture with a flick of his finger. The mission briefing itself was handwritten by, Richard was pretty sure, that very same relic the Colonel was now using to write the agreement between them.

An agreement, Richard reminded himself, that could be denied, torn up, burned, ejected into space, or shredded into oblivion if he couldn't pull off the job. The Force had never contracted him before. They had their own agents. It should not be too hard to insert an intelligence officer in civil dress. Dietrich must be desperate to be hiring a private investigator for the mission.

But the Colonel's demeanor was not desperate at all as they relentlessly attacked the flattened piece of dead tree with pen and ink. They looked completely comfortable and at ease with the utensil.

Richard returned his attention to the mission briefing. If he failed, what would happen? Would he get away with a fine? Depending on the circumstances, it could get messy. Really messy. And it wasn't only his ass on the line. It was Eddie's too. He rubbed his temple. Well, he could keep Eddie out of it. All she needed to do was get said ass—and the rest of him—to Satarim Station. She could go to Kaaloen for a sightseeing trip while he got his hands dirty trying to save the Force, and humanity in general, from embarrassment and interspecies scandal.

And he needed the job. To keep paying for parking space, for fuel, for hyper, for Eddie... Oh, who was he kidding? This felt like a challenge. And when had Richard Hart ever shied away from a challenge?

You might wonder about the high cost of a journey through hyperspace as opposed to a trip from one planet to another within a single solar system. Especially when jumping from one point in space to another many light years away is often so much faster than a trip from one planet to the next.

Obviously, you pay for the objective (and subjective as perceived by the pilot) time the journey takes, but the expenses involved are quite a lot more complicated than what can be calculated from just the temporal duration of a trip.

The cost of the fuel alone is a lot higher when a ship is catapulting itself into the depths of hyperspace as compared to a leisurely sail through normal space. And the ship in question needs regular maintenance to make sure it is in perfect condition to withstand the rigors of faster than light travel. Here, I am not talking about the unfounded superstition about strange creatures lurking in the folds of space when traversed in this way. I am merely referring to the mind-boggling speed.

In addition to that, we also have the pilot's dosage of the substance confusingly, but poignantly, called—in the jargon of spacefarers—hyper. It is not cheap in itself, and neither is a hyper pilot's license or the modifications that allow them to quickly absorb the drug. Those costs taken into consideration, along with the recently obligatory rest periods between dosages, it is no wonder that we mere mortals have to pay a substantial fee for safe transport through the galaxy.

- Alannah Jackson, *Interstellar Sightseeing 101*

6
GETTING PHYSICAL

Cold water splashed against Eddie's face, and as her mouth opened in a gasp that she didn't manage to suppress, she imagined steam rising from the meeting between the icy shower and her sweaty skin.

Her heart was still racing and her breath jagged after the run. She had gone through the entirety of the *Colibri*'s hallways twice and managed to beat her old post-hyper record by almost three seconds.

Eddie turned, placed her hands against the wall of the shower stall and leaned, stretching her muscles. Maybe it would be better to do this before hitting the shower, but she had craved that cold water so much. And she wanted to be out and dressed and not smelling like a farm animal before Richard returned from his oh-so-mysterious meeting on Stonehenge.

There were several reasons Eddie liked to exercise and push herself as much as she could. During her career as a Trans World Trading pilot, she had been pretty idle, physically speaking. She had, admittedly, let herself go. When she eventually was trashed like a grubby takeout container, she had been the unhealthy and not the fashionable kind of thin. It had actually frightened her to discover how frail she was. She couldn't run more than a few minutes if her life depended on it and might have lost a fistfight with a child back then. And she never, ever wanted to be in that place again. Didn't want to feel weak. And then there was the fact that Richard Hart was practically the poster boy of healthy physique, and hell if she wanted to feel like his inferior. He was the vision of wholesomeness in a nutshell. Well, under a layer of trendy scruff. Finally, regular physical exhaustion was a good distraction from the restlessness immediately after a jump, as well as the jitteriness that crept up on her after a couple of days clean.

She was almost looking and feeling human again when her patch alerted her to an incoming message. It was lying under the bundle of clean clothes on the bench next to the shower stall. Eddie fished it out and fastened the thin band around her wrist again. It was waterproof, but she preferred to be completely naked when she bathed. She brought up the display and looked at the new alert. Incoming chick. The feed from the ship told her it was Richard coming in at a lethargic lack of speed. He piloted like a senior citizen walking an ancient dog, so she had plenty of time to get to the nest and meet him.

Eddie shimmied into her pants, a feat made difficult by her still damp skin, slipped on a supportive tank top and stepped into her boots. She made her way through the ship, taking long gulps from her bottle of electrolyted water on the way.

The *Colibri* vibrated slightly as her outer airlock opened to admit the chick. Then once more as it closed. Eddie stopped outside the nest, looking at the screen next to the door. Richard was waiting for the room to get the proper atmospheric values before he could get out of the chick. He was holding something white in front of him and frowning at it. Eddie wondered what it was.

Finally, the doors reacted to Eddie's presence and slid apart. She strode into the nest as Richard was climbing out of the chick.

"Welcome back!" Eddie called out.

Richard looked up. "Not a scratch," he said.

"What?" Eddie asked. That was a bit of a non sequitur even if she guessed he was talking about the chick.

"That's not what you said," he realized.

"I said welcome back. But I'm glad your... um... reckless flying didn't damage the little guy," Eddie replied. "How did your mysterious meeting go? Do we have a job?"

Richard grinned. "Yes, we do," he said and held up the flimsy, white rectangle.

"Is that... paper?" Eddie asked. It looked like paper. Like a piece of genuine, perishable, ground to a pulp and bleached vegetation.

"Yes. It's the contract. I signed it with ink," he said almost reverently.

Eddie raised an eyebrow. "Wow. Did you seal it with wax too?"

"Sadly, no," Richard replied. "The Colonel didn't go quite that far."

"Why pen and paper, though?" Eddie asked.

"It's... a very delicate matter. They want to keep it off the record. Which is why we're going to have a talk about it before we go anywhere. Lunch?"

"Sure." Eddie side-eyed him as they walked through the ship to the galley. He was worried about something. Was the job dangerous? Or just complicated? What did delicate even mean? Eddie was pretty sure it wasn't going to involve zetoi calligraphy or wendek perfumes, which accounted for the two most delicate things in the entire galaxy that sprang to mind.

"Everything in this contract and everything I'm about to tell you is highly confidential," Richard began when they sat across from each other at the table in the galley, bumping into each other's knees under it.

"Wow, really? That's your opening line?" Eddie asked. "Who the hell would I even tell? I'm pretty sure I signed an NDA when I agreed to work with you in the first place. How many more precautions do you need? Enough with the stalling." She picked up her fork and twirled noodles around it.

"All right," Richard replied. "The Force suspects someone is going to a planet in the Kaaloen system for unknown reasons. Its inhabitants are sentient, but their society is, apparently, nowhere near advanced enough to be considered for the Union."

"And this 'someone' is human?" Eddie guessed.

"Yes. It would be catastrophic for our relations to the draevere if humans messed up the natural evolution of a primitive society in a system under their jurisdiction."

"Right," Eddie said, slurping her noodles thoughtfully. "So the TDF wants us to go fix it?"

"Yes... Or rather, one branch of the Force does. And not necessarily us. Only me. I need you to get me to Kaaloen system, but you can stay at Satarim Station while I—"

"Oh, come on!" Eddie scoffed, noodles flopping gracelessly from her mouth. She munched them down and swallowed. "Do you expect me to let you have all the fun? No way."

"There's a catch," Richard said. "If the draevere discover what we're doing, the Force will deny involvement. If you stay on the station or go sightseeing on Kaaloen, you will be free and clear in case there's any trouble."

"Okay," Eddie said, shrugging. "What's the mysterious planet like this time of year? I'm still coming with you. We'll just have to be careful."

Richard studied her for a moment. She trusted she looked thoroughly unimpressed by his warnings. "All right," he conceded. "You know the risk."

"Great!" Eddie clapped her hands together. "When are we leaving?"

"Tomorrow," Richard said, readily.

Eddie huffed. "We can go today, you know."

"No," Richard insisted. "We can't. Your last dose of hyper must have worn off, and I'm not authorizing two on the same day. We've been over this. Please don't argue with me."

She wanted to tell him to stuff a dose of hyper up his ass. It wasn't like she hadn't tried doubledosing before. As a TWT pilot, she had done it often enough. And that was exactly the reason she didn't have that job anymore, she reminded herself. "Fine. Tomorrow it is."

Richard nodded. "In the meantime, we can do some research. Read up on the planet and its features."

"Question," Eddie interjected. "If it's restricted, we can't exactly find a tour guide. How are we supposed to learn anything about it?"

"The draevere have their eyes on the planet. Just because no one goes there doesn't mean they haven't done a few flybys. I'm sure we can assemble enough material to do our homework."

"Yay," Eddie said flatly. "Homework."

As you undoubtedly already know, the Union is composed of a number of different sentient species of which humanity is only one. Most of us can name some of them off the top of our heads, such as the zetois, the wendek, the draevere and the åayu.

But they, too, only make up a small part of the galactic population. Like us, they are members of what is known as Category 3. Each category is made up of largely compatible species. Of course, our biologies and capabilities differ quite a lot. For instance, the wendek use subtle pheromones in addition to verbal communication, zetois can fly, and åayu are largely amphibious. Still, we can all communicate, at least partially, verbally. We all need oxygen in our atmospheres, we all have the ability to move around on legs, we all have hands with digits that can touch and grasp objects, and our bodies can withstand the same forces of gravity without being crushed.

In short, each category is a Venn diagram of compatibility. Each species within a category has characteristics that do not apply to others, but we share a lot of the same, overlapping values.

When we think about it like that, it is not strange that interaction with members of other categories doesn't take place as often, especially for a species like ours who only recently, at least from the larger perspective of universal time, was allowed to join the Union and is still getting used to being part of the interstellar community.

You might still meet individuals from other species, however. It is not unheard of for ships to have a layover on stations that don't cater to their crews' needs. So if you ever meet a person encased in an environment suit on your travels, it is most likely someone from a different Union category.

- Alannah Jackson, *Interstellar Sightseeing 101*

7
UNDERCOVER

Although Richard had never been to Satarim Station before, he was pretty sure it would feel like every other space station. Or at least every other Category 3 station. He had visited a couple of other categories in the Union, and the most positive thing he could call that experience was 'interesting'. The Union had plenty of reasons to fit its member species into compatible categories. How was a human being supposed to interact meaningfully with a representative of a species that looked like a gelatinous blob, communicated solely through telepathy, and who moved around by floating through an atmosphere that wasn't breathable to humans? Richard, having had respect drilled into him during his early military career, knew that to the gelatinous blob, he was the alien whose body was strange at best and repulsive at worst and who couldn't even survive in a proper atmosphere. No thanks. Richard would stick to Cat 3 if at all possible.

The moment they stepped out of the chick and onto the docks, Eddie stumbled. She swore under her breath and quickly caught herself.

"You okay?" Richard asked.

Under normal circumstances, he had no trouble finding clothes that fit the bill. He knew what clients expected. He knew how subtle military associations that people connected with reliability and seriousness made them trust him. But for this mission, he wanted to appear as inconspicuous as possible. Tourists were as different as zetois and wendek, so it ought to be easy. Yet, he spent an embarrassing amount of time selecting something from the *Colibri*'s printer menu because he not only wanted to look like a tourist, he wanted to look like a civilian, but not the civilian he actually was, trying to look inconspicuously like a tourist.

Eddie clearly didn't give a damn about projection. She had a style, and she stuck with it like her life depended on it. Right now, she was wearing pants so tight that they would endanger reproductive abilities for someone with a different set of genitals, and her usual ecoleather jacket that was too short to offer any kind of real protection against cold. They had both stashed some more planet-appropriate clothing in the chick, so they could take off as soon as possible.

At the moment, though, they were both wearing grav boots instead of their usual footwear.

"I'm fine," Eddie said, straightening up. "These boots are just..."

Richard had to agree. Because of the lower gravity on the draeveres' home world—they were taller and built more heavily than humans—and on the station, Richard and Eddie would both be bouncing around like animated balloon animals if they didn't add weight to their bodies. And the best way to do that was a pair of grav boots with a setting corresponding to human needs.

"Well, let's get to work, then," Richard said and had to stifle a yawn. He wasn't tired. But the air had slightly lower oxygen levels than the average human was used to. It wasn't an actual problem unless you had a compromised respiratory system or were an overenthusiastic fan attending a crowded concert in a draever system. For a while, the human news media had a field day calling draever popular music addictive and dangerous until a sensible person told them that the only reason human attendees had a tendency to faint during live concerts was the difference in atmospheric conditions, and not that the music made humans more hysterical than any other music.

"Yep, see you later," Eddie agreed.

"Three Earth hours from now," Richard reminded her.

"Yes, Mom," Eddie said and turned away from him to begin her research.

Richard was still not sure involving his pilot in this particular mission was such a great idea. But she had insisted, and two sets of eyes and ears were better than one. Or, well, two sets of eyes and one set of ears with the proper connection to a brain. And Eddie knew what she was getting into. Right now, her job was to take a look at the public docking records, determine whether the suspects' ship was currently here, and if so, if their chick had been left in the nest or gone somewhere. It should be inconspicuous enough. Anyone could look at flight itineraries. Eddie would simply pretend to be a pilot with a hyper addiction looking for work. So no pretending at all, apart from the last bit.

Richard's own task was a tad more precarious. He made his way out of the docking area, through the commercial passageways of Satarim Station, past food stands and souvenir shops, avoiding the inner rings of the station where the authorities would be located.

Colonel Dietrich had included a few leads to follow in the briefing material. The best one was a draever called Liyaa who operated in the underground, a concept even more metaphorical on a space station than anywhere else. Supposedly, this Liyaa was conducting some kind of illegal business having to do with helping people go off the grid, which was precisely the sort of thing Richard's quarries needed. And Richard himself, as it were.

So Richard went to the small bar that allegedly was Liyaa's chosen place of operations. Not that there was any guarantee the draever would be there, but Richard had a few stills of her and a pretty good eye for seedy characters. The place was dimly lit and crowded already at this time in the station's designated afternoon. A silent wall display ran a loop of clips advertising various alcoholic beverages that matched the smells of the premises perfectly. A popular song by a draever band played through speakers, the percussion changing in speed and volume as the sound bounced around the room. Richard didn't think the music could be too loud for people to be able to talk in a comfortable way, but as it was, he didn't much care.

Richard headed straight for the bar. He made a show of badly concealing his scanning of the premises. Brought a bit of a nervous edge to his movements. Not too much. Just enough to make the clientele wonder. But he needn't worry. He was the only human in this place. A zetoi sat with what Richard assumed were two friends at a table, looking completely out of place, but apart from them, everybody was draever.

"Yes?" the bartender asked. He was a good head taller than Richard—who was by no means short for a human male. With a shoulder width that Richard would have to wear infantry issue combat shoulder pads under his shirt to achieve, the bartender looked even more intimidating as most draevere did on first impression. Richard generally liked draevere better when they sat down. No wonder the Force had panicked and launched into that disastrous soldier enhancement project some years ago.

"I'll have a beer," Richard said.

"What kind?" the bartender asked, holding out the palm of his hand questioningly.

"Whatever you recommend," Richard decided. Every species had some variant of beer. That was universal. Sure, whatever was in the glass the bartender was filling would not taste much like the kind found in human settlements, but it was a neutral enough alcoholic beverage. Enough in a glass for Richard to nurse it for a good while and not too high an alcohol percentage, even in the draever variant, to get him too drunk to carry out his job.

Equipped with beer, caution, and vigilance, Richard retreated to a table as a pair of draevere departed.

He sat down, projecting the air of a person who wanted to merge with the wall behind him, but who was also looking for someone. He tried to spot the draever he was looking for in the bad lighting of the barroom. On the stills, Liyaa had no obvious style, alterations or other features. That meant the draever to Richard's right who sported a discount artificial hand wasn't her. Neither was the one with the flashy clothes laughing at something the zetoi said.

It turned out that he did not have to be the one to initiate contact. A woman came out of the shadows on the far side of the room and aimed for Richard's table. Richard pretended to be surprised to see her.

"Hello, human," the draever said in Standard. She was middle height for a female draever which made her taller than the bartender. Her scales looked a little on the dull side. Not oiled like some of her species preferred them.

"Ah, hello," Richard returned, frowning up at the draever. Oh yes, this was Liyaa all right.

"What brings you here?"

"I'm just having a drink," Richard said, mock-defensively. "I'm meeting someone." And then, theatrically under his breath, "I hope."

"Maybe I can help you," Liyaa said, smiling, which always had an unnerving effect to someone of a human persuasion because a draever's reptilian, lipless mouth stretched too wide and showed many sharp teeth. "May I sit? My name is Liyaa, by the way. What is yours?"

Richard made an inviting gesture. "Oh," he breathed. "Then you're the one I'm looking for! I'm Arthur," he added.

"Delighted to meet you, Arthur," Liyaa said. "Now, what can I do for you?"

"I hear you can arrange a little trip off the grid, as it were," Richard said in a low voice.

A smirk twitched at the corner of Liyaa' mouth. "Who told you that?"

"Someone who has an interest in... unexplored territory." Richard raised his eyebrows suggestively. "Like me."

Liyaa' inner eyelids closed and opened again in the draever equivalent of a nod. "I see. Did this someone also tell you what I charge?"

"Not in detail," Richard said. He had no clue.

Liyaa told him.

On a hunch, Richard shook his head. He could pay. With the Colonel's units. But he had a feeling he shouldn't appear desperate. Liyaa might get suspicious. "That's steep," he said. "Knock off 20 percent, or I will find someone else."

"Someone else," Liyaa scoffed. "Please."

"Satarim is a big station," Richard said and raised his glass to look at Liyaa over the rim.

"I can take five percent off," the draever said. "I'm not going any lower."

Richard sipped his beer slowly, stalling, staring Liyaa down. When the alien showed no signs of cracking, he sighed. "Fine. Five percent. So how exactly are we doing this?"

"There is an antiques shop in one of the inner rings of the station," Liyaa began. "They have a big collection of pre-Helaaren art. You buy any of it for the price we've agreed on and hand over the wares to me."

Clever, Richard had to admit. Like the Colonel's quaint pen and paper trick, this scheme was a good way to avoid any traces of the transaction. Liyaa probably exported the goods through some other company, possibly even more expensively. "I see. And how do I get what I pay for?"

"Upon payment, I give you two clearance codes. You take out your chick, tell station control you are headed to a mining colony on Enraa, give them the first code and leave. You will have a Kaaloen five-day window to go where you want and come back. Then use the second code to verify your identity and purpose. Clean and simple."

It was. Richard had to give her that. "How exactly—"

Liyaa made a dismissive flick of her wrist. "No. You don't need to know how or why it works. And I don't need to know where you are going or what you intend to do there. Like I said, clean and simple."

Richard nodded. Well, his job wasn't to dismantle whatever shady business Liyaa was doing here. It was to get to Motarpria, find the trespassers, extract them, and bring them to Dietrich. Nothing else. "All right," he conceded. "I have a few preparations to make. How about—"

Liyaa smiled. "Meet me in front of The Green Gothaa in three station hours, and we will exchange our wares."

Richard had no idea what the Green Gothaa was, but he imagined it must be another bar or restaurant or shop. Shouldn't be too hard to locate. "The Green Gothaa," he repeated. "I will see you then." He downed the rest of his beer and stood up.

Approaching a planet—always amazing as it stands out from the darkness of space. Even more so with a planet that has only just been cleared for interstellar travelers, etc.

First impressions of Motarpria from space: One moon, boring? M is small. Northern hemisphere white (ice/snow - glaciers?).

Three major landmasses. A couple of wide rivers cutting through. 50% ocean?

Getting closer: Traces of sentient life (eg lights/roads). Most densely populated around the equator. Scattered settlements further north too.

Glittering like diamonds, the pureness of the landscape below as we fly closer and the chick prepares for landing.

Beautiful mountain range (find out its local name!) with foothills and plains of untouched snow. Some trees/other vegetation, swathed in a cape of pure white. Herd of animals cutting through the landscape, oblivious to the approaching aliens.

(No defined landing spaces yet. Probably will be there when the planet is cleared? Check up on this later!)

Landing in the pristine snow. Stepping outside, breathing in the clear, cold air, unpolluted by civilization/cities/technology (except for the smell and heat of the chick, better leave that out).

Remember: notes on the climate/appropriate clothing!

- Alannah Jackson's private travel notes

8
A CLASH OF IDEALS

In retrospect, Alannah knew she should have asked questions. About the crew. About the tourists, for lack of a better term, who were going with them. About the mysterious equipment loaded onto the oversized chick. About the layover at Satarim Station where no one was allowed to leave the ship. About—Oh, about all the damn things she had not asked about. Sure, she had politely inquired if any of the others were writers too, but she had not pursued the matter when they said they were tourists. Where was her sense of investigative journalism? It wasn't like her to be that stupid. And she hadn't really been, had she? She made the choice not to ask those questions because she wanted this job so badly. She was so proud that Lisa Boucher handpicked her for it. She had trusted that it was somehow okay even though Motarpria was a restricted world.

And now... Now she was here. Now she was going to have to ask all the questions she had neglected before. Because they had just finished setting up a shelter by the chick, and the expedition leader was addressing them all, holding a kinetic rifle that could probably bring down an armored gothaa or shoot a hole in the pelso plating of a ship.

The leader of the group swiped at his patch, and a display on the wall of the shelter lit up. It showed a still of a group of animals. They were hexapods with shaggy fur and what appeared to be tusks protruding from their jaws. One of the creatures had a clump of snow stuck on there. Alannah assumed they were mammals though she had no real way of knowing. One of them was bigger than the others and had darker fur. The small ones were white and really fluffy, like piles of snow themselves. It was impossible to tell how big they really were on the backdrop of a barren, snowy landscape. The image faded into a map of, Alannah assumed, the immediate area around the camp.

"I am aware," the leader of the expedition, Ernest, said, "that for some of you, this is your first safari. But you all have some kind of firearm license, so learning how to handle this bad boy shouldn't be a problem." He held up the rifle.

Everybody in the audience nodded and gave various answers in the affirmative. Well, everybody but Alannah.

"Excuse me," she said, waving for Ernest's attention.

"Ahh, Miss Jackson," he said, smiling at her. "I am aware you don't have a license. But since you are our special guest, I think we can make an exception if you want to participate."

"Thank you," Alannah said automatically, "but I would like to ask why you think weapons are necessary. As observers, we shouldn't attract any attention from—"

The expedition leader's smile turned into a grin. Several of the others laughed.

"—from predators," she finished, louder. "We aren't meant to interact at all."

"Do you think this is a beach holiday?" someone asked.

Ernest coughed. "Miss Jackson... This is a safari. A hunting trip."

"What?" Alannah spluttered. She scanned the crowd. No one else appeared to be even the slightest bit surprised. "But— But you can't possibly have permission— We aren't here to—"

His smile didn't falter. "Oh, yes we are. Starlite only asked us to take you along so you can write your little guides or whatever it is that you do. I'm just offering you an opportunity to join the fun."

"What— What are you even hunting?" Alannah asked, turning to the display on the wall as it faded back into the still of the hexapods. "No—" Her voice broke. "No!" Not those adorable, little creatures. Ethically speaking, it didn't matter if the prey was cute or repulsive to her individual idea of aesthetics, but she instinctively responded warmly to those woolly cuties.

"Oh yes." Ernest radiated glee. To Alannah, his expression looked sinister. She had spent her whole life grappling with the fact that morals and ethics and rules were not the same to everybody. That something she took for granted as perfectly okay to do could be disrespectful to a wendek, or that something she would classify as despicable was as natural as breathing to a draever. Nothing in the vast universe was truly universal. That was her takeaway from years of researching and experiencing other cultures. But— This guy was human, dammit. The whole group was, and no matter how flexible she tried to keep her mind, hunting animals for sport was not okay. White fluffballs or not.

Alannah spun to face the rest of the group. "Did you know?" she asked. "Are you okay with this?"

"Lady, it's what we paid for," one of the tourists said. They looked thoroughly amused with her objections.

"It's not like shooting a couple of them will lead to extinction or anything," another reasoned, shrugging.

Alannah shook her head. "That is bullshit!" she said. "Killing other creatures for sport is— Look, it doesn't even matter. This planet is restricted! We are supposed to be observers only and—"

"Who the fuck pays for looking at the landscape?" another of the expedition team members asked. He was the pilot, a lean man with a balding head and a cynical set to his mouth.

Alannah opened her mouth, but Ernest's hand closed around her arm. "Miss Jackson," he said, "if I may have a word with you in private."

She jerked away from him. "Don't Miss Jackson me!" she said. "Everybody should hear this! I'm not going to stand by and let you..." She trailed off. Twelve pairs of eyes were staring at her in various states of dismay or anger. Twelve pairs of eyes all attached to heavily-armed individuals who were preparing to march out there and murder animals for sport. Maybe continuously pissing them off was not such a bright idea. After all, what was stopping them from turning those rifles on Alannah? Was she the sort of person who would die for her ideals? Yes! No... Maybe. But it wouldn't make a dent in reality here. It would be a statement that no one ever saw because legally speaking—officially speaking—none of them was even here. Not her, not the two expedition leaders, not the pilot, and not the nine tourists. It might be better to shut up now and come up with... something.

Ernest grabbed her arm again. "Jessica," he told his colleague, "carry on the introduction for a bit, okay? Niels, give me a hand." He didn't wait for confirmation from either of them before coercing the troublesome writer out of this compartment of the shelter.

"Where are you taking me?" Alannah asked, trying not to let her voice quaver as her mind played a macabre feature involving her blood splattering on the crisp, white snow... her mourning family never knowing where she had gone.

"I don't want you in there creating a bad mood," Ernest said. "If you don't want to come along, you'll just have to wait out our trip."

"Oh," Alannah said, breathing a sigh of relief.

He motioned for her to enter the next compartment of the shelter and then to sit down on one of the chairs in the temporary living room. "Give me your handcuffs," he said to the other man.

"Are you sure about this?" the pilot, Niels, asked as he unclipped a set of handcuffs from his belt that left Alannah wondering why the hell they had brought those on the trip. To handcuff the animals? Or to deal with people who suddenly backed out...

Ernest pushed Alannah onto the chair and closed one of the cuffs around her wrist. "Do you have another suggestion?" he asked as he guided the chain around the chair behind Alannah's back.

"It *is* a very cold climate," the pilot began. "And the weather might change unexpectedly. If she happened to wander outside and got herself lost in a blizzard..."

"No," Ernest said sharply. "I won't stand for that. We are not killing off a member of our own expedition."

Alannah felt trapped between her own ideals that all life was equal and utter relief that she wasn't about to be murdered.

"Her publisher is our main sponsor," he continued, rendering Alannah's assumptions about the potential goodness of his heart pretty obsolete. He closed the second handcuff and stepped back. "You stay here, little miss."

"It's not like I have a choice now, do I?" Alannah muttered.

They left her, presumably going back to the rest of the group. Ten minutes later, feet crunched the snow outside. Commotion, instructions being shouted, annoyingly upbeat remarks about it being a good day for hunting, and so on. The voices grew fainter as the poaching party put distance between themselves and the camp. By the sound of it, they were going in the direction the map had shown. Toward the mountain range and the plains below that Alannah had seen when they flew in to land.

She sat for a while listening. Then she uttered a string of curses that would have made the most seasoned pilot in the docks of Yellowstone blush. She even made a few wordless, growling screams for good, frustrated, measure.

After that, she sat for a while, contemplating her options. There were precious few of them. She wiggled her fingers. Then her toes. How long were they going to be gone for, anyway? No less than five hours at the very least. Five hours was fine. She could wait. But it might also be ten hours, she supposed. That would no doubt result in a sore butt, but that wasn't so bad. As long as she didn't get an itch on her nose or something.

"Why are you such an idiot?" she groaned five seconds later when she did, indeed, have an itch on her nose. She craned her neck, trying to rub her nose on her shoulder, but it didn't really work. A lot of scrunching up her face later, she gave up and decided to think about something else.

The first subject that presented itself then was, naturally, what the poachers would do with her when they returned. Did they realize that nothing kept her from telling the authorities, human or draever, about this venture? Nothing apart from the fact that she would be incriminating herself, but... Would they threaten her in order to make her keep her mouth shut? Or would they eventually come to the conclusion that the best option was accidentally, quote unquote, leaving her on this planet, or just shoving her out the airlock into the vast airlessness of space?

Alannah closed her eyes and decided to try meditating for a bit.

Although they are usually small compared to even the tiny Apodiformes class spaceships, chicks are sturdy and maneuverable vessels in their own right. They may depend on the nest of their mother ship for energy, but once charged, they are fully capable of undertaking interplanetary journeys.

The bigger the ship, the larger chicks it can carry. Smaller ships usually only have one or two chicks in their nests whereas large ones sometimes fit in 10 or even 20. Most private ship owners prefer the cost-effectiveness of chicks with room for no more than the pilot and between one and five passengers. But you will find more spacious chicks on some Terran Defense Force ships and tourist cruisers where the capacity is needed.

Chicks are meant to ferry passengers not only between their mother ship and a space station, but also from stations to their respective planets, and through a solar system from one planet to another. So it follows that they are safe and their hulls covered in pelso plating that can withstand radiation and get them through an atmosphere without a scratch. If you have ever traveled beyond your home, be it to a planet or a station, you've likely seen that all chicks have retractable wings that make them useful even when they are not in the vacuum of space.

- Alannah Jackson, *Interstellar Sightseeing 101*

9

SHE IS BEAUTY, SHE IS GRACE

Eddie Macías had so definitely not become a pilot to fly chicks over long distances. Apart from takeoff and landing, it was as boring as a zetoi opera. Though zetoi operas only took four hours before you were off the hook. An ex girlfriend of hers was into that kind of thing and once forced Eddie to sit through one. Not only did she not want to be distracted, which was a bummer because the only reason Eddie had agreed to watch the opera was that she'd assumed, "Wanna come over to my place and watch a zetoi opera?" was a euphemism, but the ex also insisted on quizzing Eddie on her opinions afterward. "There was a lot of singing and wing flapping" was, apparently, not considered a satisfactory review. It wasn't musical incompatibility that broke them up, but it certainly didn't help.

"Shouldn't you concentrate on flying?" Richard asked from his seat beside Eddie. He was leaning forward a bit to be able to see her mouth when she spoke, which felt intrusive when they sat next to, and not across from, each other. But neither of them could do anything about that.

"Why?" Eddie asked. The chick's display and controls were right there in front of her, and her gaze returned to them every few moments. She'd had to do all of three course corrections so far.

"I don't find it terribly comforting that you are looking more at your game than where we're going."

"And I," Eddie replied, swiping her fingers rapidly across the projected patch display, "don't find it terribly comforting that you don't think I can multitask. Richard, we're in space going at sub lightspeed. There is literally nothing for me to do."

"I don't think that word means what you think it does," he said.

"I know what literally means!" Eddie huffed.

"I'm talking about multitask," Richard replied.

Eddie blinked. "What?"

"It means doing several things badly at the same time," he replied. "My point is there are asteroids and—"

"Really?" Eddie interrupted him. "*You* are going to lecture *me*, a professional spaceship pilot, about the dangers of space?"

At least the man had the decency to look sheepish.

"Besides, multitasking may mean that to people like you, but I still have a bit of hyper in my system."

Richard nodded, defeated by the facts. And then added, "Obviously."

Eddie almost demanded to know what he meant, but she knew. Her fingers' speed on the game controls, her ability to play while keeping up a conversation, while paying attention to the chick's controls, while considering buying a hat of the sort private investigators always wore in historical crime shows just to piss Richard off... Her slightly too rapid speech, her inability to look at one thing for more than a split-second. And her annoyance with having to go at a speed that made getting out and walking seem like a thrilling option.

So far, their mission for the mysterious TDF Colonel was going smoothly. While Eddie had verified that another human-owned ship was indeed docked at Satarim and that its chick had apparently flown off in the direction of a mining colony on one of Kaaloen's moons half an Earth day ahead of them, Richard had done some shady business in a bar. He was sometimes so self-righteous that she forgot he was also qualified at shady businesses. Most soldiers she met were straight-laced, and in his own way, Richard was too. But he had been an intelligence officer, and that was probably what gave him a bit of... Perspective, Eddie decided. The kind of perspective that made him hire a former TWT pilot despite her reputation. Someday, she was going to get him real drunk and give her the juicy details of his life before he was sacked.

A couple of hours later, the system's fourth planet was looming ahead. It was a fairly small one with only one tiny moon in orbit. Clouds were hanging out in the atmosphere, and the oceans glittered blue in the light of the local star.

"Are we close enough to scan for traces of their chick?" Richard asked.

"Just a moment." On a world like this, it should be simple to pick up signs of chick activity. The natives didn't have space faring craft yet, so there would be no energy signatures in the atmosphere except for what their targets put out.

Eddie wondered what they were doing. It could be anything from smuggling pre-Union planetary art all over the galaxy to doing illegal scientific research. Or worse. "We have a match," she said and routed the results to Richard's patch.

"Well, that's one thing confirmed. They are definitely here," Richard replied.

"Yeah, job's done. Let's go back and tell your Colonel," Eddie said.

"Sorry, what?" He hadn't been looking at her.

"Nothing," she said. "Where do you want me to take us down?"

Richard was studying the representation of the planet on his patch display, moving it around with his fingers. "Around... Here," he said and sent the coordinates back to her.

"All right. Hello again, passengers," Eddie said as she swiped the game display away and devoted her full attention to the chick. "Please fasten your seat belts. We will be landing in just a few minutes." Not that anyone had a choice about the seat belts. The moment she initiated the proper landing protocols, sturdy restraints emerged from every occupied seat in the chick and pulled their occupants into a tight hug that would last until the moment the tiny vessel was sitting safely on the ground.

The chick's wing unfolded for stability, and the ship shot through the atmosphere like a particularly smug comet unable to burn up before it landed. Beneath them, because when you entered the atmosphere, directions like up and down began to make sense again, the planet grew steadily bigger, filling up the whole viewscreen. They were coming in on the day side of Motarpria.

The energy traces led them to what looked like an arctic region of the planet. It was supposed to have temperatures similar to that of Earth, and they had both assumed humans would land in a temperate zone, but this... It wasn't near the north pole, but the ground was covered in snow. Good thing they had stocked the chick for every eventuality.

Eddie scanned for a suitable spot to land. No native settlements were situated close by. Could be the reason the others had landed here. That meant Eddie didn't have to worry about anything but the distance to the other chick. She located a nice place with smooth ground and steered for it. She had been afraid the landing would be bumpy with the lack of a designated space for it, but this—

Touchdown. A perfect one that sent only minimal tremors through the chick's structure. Eddie hit the brakes. And nothing much happened.

"Eddie?" Richard asked.

She didn't reply. The chick was sliding along the ground. Because the ground, Eddie realized, wasn't packed soil covered by snow. There was ice under there. "Hold on!" she said, unnecessarily. On the nav display, warnings flared to life. They were coming up on obstacles. Eddie gritted her teeth and swung the controls to the right, swerving around a small mountain.

Richard was silent. A less sensible person might have demanded to know what was happening again or have shouted warnings at her, but he knew his odds of survival were proportionate to letting her do her job in peace.

Her hyper-enhanced senses came in handy when Eddie had to make a sharp turn left and then right again. But then a mountain range too solid and too big for her to swerve around filled up the viewscreen. Shit. She pushed hard at the controls, causing the chick to turn 180 degrees on its own axis. It kept sliding. Eddie ignited the thrusters that were meant to propel the chick forward on a take-off ramp, effectively putting stop to the chick's motion. It came to rest ten meters from the stony mountain face.

"Thank you for flying with *Colibri* Airlines," Eddie said, trying to sound like she'd had the situation under control the entire time, which was not exactly a lie. Not... exactly. "We wish you a pleasant day."

The restraints retracted without a comment.

Richard, of course, did not. "What the hell just happened?"

"I decided to live out my childhood dream and be a figure skating princess," Eddie said. "Did you enjoy it?"

"You almost crashed us into an iceberg!" Richard shouted as if she was the one with a hearing impairment.

"Almost being the operative word here," Eddie retorted, pushing the command that would fold up the chick's wings again. "I didn't expect ice, okay? Just be happy you have one of TWT's former ace pilots at your disposal." And be happy that you don't get motion sick, she didn't add. She was also really happy he didn't. It usually wasn't a problem in space, but some people really couldn't stomach, literally, entering an atmosphere or a bumpy landing.

"I'd hate to see a bad pilot land here," Richard muttered. A strand of hair had fallen out of his carefully constructed hairdo, and he pushed it back into place. Despite his words, though, that was the only thing about him that appeared ruffled.

Before they left the *Colibri*, Richard and Eddie had stashed a pile of clothes in the chick. They had studied the planet's conditions. The gravity and atmosphere were even closer to their preferred specs than the draevere's. That could be one of the reasons it was humans who went there, and not any other species... Oh, who was she kidding? Eddie knew perfectly well why it was humans and not anyone else. That was because humans were the stupidest kind of rebellious opportunists. End of story.

Well, even knowing the general conditions of Motarpria left Richard and Eddie with a pretty big margin for error. They hadn't known where on this dirtball their targets had landed and therefore had no idea how the local weather or climate would look. They had bundled up enough clothes to account for several eventualities. Clearly, they would have no use for flimsy tank tops or comfortable running shoes here.

Eddie stripped to her underwear and pulled on what looked and felt like a full-body sock. It clung to her like a second skin, but despite the thin material, whatever it was; Eddie was a pilot, not a fabric expert, it had a high level of insulation against the cold they would meet outside.

She turned to see Richard slip on his own weird sock, the hair on his head protruding from the high neck somehow still in near perfect condition.

They put on the rest of their clothes, placed their patches on top of their sleeves so they didn't have to expose their skin to access them, and then gathered their equipment.

"Ready?" Richard asked, as he hoisted his backpack onto his shoulders, giving her a look that suggested he was accessing whether she had put on her clothes right. Control freak.

Eddie nodded.

They stood crammed together in the small decon area by the hatch. Eddie squeezed her eyes shut against the dry huff of decontaminant and then waited for the chick's suction system to do its thing. It only took a minute.

Richard opened the hatch. Cold seeped into the chick. He put on his gloves. "Chilly."

"We're going to freeze our asses off," Eddie said.

"No," he said, reasonably. "Our insulation suits will keep us warm. Especially so when we start moving. Your ass will be fine."

Maybe, but Eddie hated being cold. She'd take too hot over too cold any day. "So what now?" she asked, although she knew the answer already.

Richard stepped outside, testing the ground before putting his weight down, an action that was pretty redundant since they had landed several tons of spacecraft on the ice a few minutes ago. "Now we track down the other chick, get documentation that they are here, and see if we might be able to apprehend them and leave without a trace."

"Well, yes," Eddie said and followed him outside. Sure, they had insulation, but not on their faces. If nothing else did, her nose was going to freeze off before this mission was over. "Should we... cover the chick or something?" she asked. "In case of natives..."

They stood looking at the chick for a moment. They had arrived in what Eddie estimated to be late local morning, and the landscape was glittering in the sunlight. The chick stood out like a big, blueish grey lump of metal against the white snow, which it was. It had plowed long skidmarks into the ground from their point of touchdown to the place it was sitting now.

"There isn't supposed to be any settlements nearby," Richard said. "Let's just get out of here."

Eddie shrugged. It wasn't like she wanted to spend hours turning the chick into a giant snowman that would be at least as conspicuous as a spacecraft. "Maybe it'll snow some more."

"Maybe. Remember where we parked," Richard added and began to march away from the chick.

"Yeah, gonna be a real hassle when the parking lot is this crowded," Eddie said to his back.

The landscape they were facing looked a lot like the poles of Earth. Or, like Eddie imagined them. Lots of snow crunching under her feet and treacherous ice underneath. Mountains, icebergs... Completely untouched by civilization. Very idyllic. Kind of beautiful. She hoped they would be able to find their fellow humans and get off this planet soon.

Okay... Did I get it? I think so.

Leave it to me to have my dictation tool handy on my patch and nothing useful like... like an emergency beacon of some kind... Not that anyone would pick it up here...

Right. So... If you are listening to this, I'm probably d—

Scratch that.

My name is Alannah Jackson. I'm a travel guide writer, and I fucked up. Spectacularly. I was contracted by my publisher Starlite Planetary Guides to go on a preliminary trip to the planet Motarpria in the Kaaloen system ahead of its inclusion in the Union. Recording this, I am handcuffed to a chair in the camp while the—

Battery low.

What, now?

Battery low. Please recharge your patch to ensure uninterrupted use. Battery low.

Oh, you are fucking kidding me, you useless piece of s—

- Alannah Jackson's private travel notes, dictation

10

SURPRISE ALLIES

The other landing party had made no effort to conceal their presence. It endlessly annoyed Richard that they were cocky enough to leave their chick in plain view, but he knew he ought to be happy about it. It made his and Eddie's job that much easier. Besides, they had done the same.

Right now, Richard and Eddie were hidden behind a convenient outcropping of snow-covered rocks that gave them an excellent view of the scene ahead. They were wearing visors that could switch on various overlays when needed.

The chick was sitting heavily in the snow. Any signs of its landing there was nearly gone. There must have been a snowfall before Richard and Eddie arrived. Behind the chick, a structure was sticking up and out. It looked like one of those expensive tents that were practically biomes in their own right. It could be divided into rooms, creating living space, a kitchen, and a rudimentary bathroom. At least the ones Richard had stayed in during training missions worked like that.

Eddie said something, and Richard turned to her.

"Well, at least we now know something about our target," she said.

"Which is?" Richard prompted, although he assumed they had reached the same conclusions about the finances required to pull off something like their targets' illegal camping trip.

"Either it's someone with a very small dick, or they needed to transport a lot of people."

Richard raised an eyebrow. "Will I regret asking?"

"Probably," Eddie said and answered anyway, "Look at the size and shape of that chick. I mean, that's not a chick. It's a full-blown cock. That's overcompensation if I ever saw it. Unless they actually need that much space. Personally, I hope it's just someone with a very small dick."

"Hm," Richard replied, noncommittally, refusing to let Eddie's bad jokes interfere with his job. But she was right; The chick would be able to fit in twenty people at least, and he too hoped they wouldn't have to deal with that many. He touched the side of his visor, and the image changed from plain view to a more tactically convenient one. It took a moment for his eyes to adjust to the overlay showing heat signatures. He could make out two distinct sources. They were both stationary, but... He focused on one of them. The red overlay did not pulse or otherwise change. A living being would, at least, breathe and shift their position once in a while. Richard moved his gaze to the other one. It was situated a handful of paces away from the first red blob. And on closer inspection, he could clearly see the fluctuations. "How many targets?" he asked, turning to Eddie again. The red overlay on her looked nightmarish this close up. She'd been complaining about the cold, but clearly she still retained perfectly normal body heat.

"Two," she replied. Like him, she was watching the camp through her visor. "Both immobile."

"Just one. The other one is a heater," Richard replied.

"Then why the fuck did you ask me?"

"To make sure I didn't miss anything."

Eddie rolled her eyes, which enhanced the uncanny spectacle through the visor. "What if we both miscounted?"

"Unlikely," Richard said and turned off the overlay again. "Let's take them into custody. Stay behind me."

Eddie mumbled something that was no doubt an insult.

Richard ignored her and unholstered his dart gun. Even with the relatively low charges loaded, he hoped he wouldn't need it, but it was better to assert his authority right away than start a conversation that might turn nasty with one of their targets. Especially since it was reasonable to assume the person had been left behind to guard the camp.

He gestured for Eddie to stay behind him and didn't wait for confirmation before he began to move. There was this thing about Eddie where she would be argumentative as hell just for the sake of it, to annoy him or because she genuinely believed she was right. That would be a serious liability on a job if not for the fact that she never, ever bickered when he issued an order. Her obstinacy was a switch, Richard thought, that Eddie knew exactly when to turn on and off. He might wish she turned it off more frequently, but at least he knew she always did when it counted.

The snow crunched softly under their boots as they edged closer and moved around the chick. The tent was a sturdy structure that could probably withstand a blizzard if needed. Its opening was sealed, which made sense, but also complicated matters a little. Richard turned and mimicked stabbing and ripping open the flap.

Eddie nodded, holstered her gun and unsheathed a military grade combat knife at her thigh. For a pilot, she was always remarkably well-equipped for violence. But then, she was a pilot working for Richard Hart. Standing by the side of the entrance, Eddie quickly plunged the blade into the thick material with one hand, sliced and tore at it with the other for quick entry.

Richard stepped through the rip, both hands clasped firmly around his own firearm. "Don't move!" he barked, first in English and then in Standard, in the sort of voice he'd use to order enemy soldiers to stand down.

The person inside the tent did, indeed, not move. She did, however, make a small, startled shriek. She was sitting on a chair, and before he could properly assess her circumstances, Richard continued in both Standard and English, "Keep your hands where I can see them!"

The woman shook her head in a cloud of bouncy, purple hair. "I would love to," she replied in English. She still looked terrified. "But it's going to be a problem."

Oh. Richard realized why. The woman on the chair was not a sentinel on watch duty. She was handcuffed to said chair.

"Please don't shoot," she added.

"I won't unless you give me a reason," Richard said.

Eddie stepped through the opening in the tent behind him and made an exclamation that might have been, "what the fuck?" or "what the actual fuck?" judging by her tone and usual repertoire of exclamations.

"Who are you?" the woman asked. She was sensibly dressed in thick, insulated pants and a comfortable-looking jacket. Her whole outfit was a bluish white, perhaps to blend into the landscape, and contrasted with her dark skin.

"Where is the rest of your party?" Richard demanded.

"They went hunting."

Hunting, huh? "When will they be back?"

"I don't know. Tonight, probably. Who are you?" she insisted.

"Why were you left here?" Richard continued to ignore her question.

The woman's mouth closed, and she glanced from Richard to Eddie and back again. Then she seemed to reach a conclusion. "We had a disagreement. I thought we were only here to observe, but what they are doing is a lot more than that. I didn't want any part of it. If you are here to stop them, you have my full cooperation. I... think we're on the same side."

Richard looked at Eddie to see what she made of this.

She made a half shrug. "Do you know where they went?" she asked.

"I have a general idea, at least. I'll help you find them. The only problem..." She tugged at her restraints and made a face.

"Why don't you tell us exactly why you are here and what happened before we decide on anything?" Richard asked.

The woman's face twisted up in pain. "I would love to, but... Can you please get me out of these cuffs first? I really, really have to pee, and peeing your pants in a sub-zero climate is an extremely bad idea."

"I'll have a look." Richard approached her and bent to examine the handcuffs. "Eddie?" he asked. He might have something handy in his backpack too, but she was more deft with old-fashioned locks than he was. A fact that always made him avoid thinking of what she had been doing in the time between being fired from the TWT and meeting him.

Eddie holstered her combat knife and took Richard's place, kneeling on the floor behind the woman. She made a soft pondering kind of noise and retrieved a handy kit from a pocket.

"Your name is Eddie?" the woman asked.

Eddie replied something Richard couldn't see.

"I'm Alannah," the woman continued. "And you?"

"Richard," he supplied. After all, it might calm her down a bit and would do nothing to jeopardize their mission to tell her.

"It's a pleasure to meet both of you," Alannah said, trying for a smile. "I mean... probably."

The lock made a definitive click, and Eddie yanked it open.

"Thank you," Alannah said, visibly relieved. "I won't be a minute. The sanitary facilities are in there," she added, pointing to the partition in the corner of the tent.

"Go ahead," Richard said. He watched her retreat, trying to make up his mind about her. She probably was on their side as she claimed, but she was still on a restricted planet...

Eddie was putting her tools back into her pocket.

"Nice work," Richard said.

"Sure." She looked up at him and mouthed, "Do we trust her?"

"At the moment, at least," he replied.

Eddie nodded in the direction Alannah had gone. "And you're not just saying that because she's pretty?" she mouthed.

"No," Richard said in a low voice, "they could not possibly have left her here in anticipation of luring us in the wrong direction. I don't know why she's here in the first place, but at this point, she'll help us." He smirked. "You think she's pretty."

Eddie rolled her eyes. "Shut up," she said.

Richard wiped the smile off his face. "Don't get too attached. We still don't know anything about her."

Eddie's undoubtedly snotty retort was cut short when Alannah returned to their area of the tent again.

She smiled and sighed. "Thank you. Now I can think," she said.

"Hopefully you can also talk," Richard suggested.

The smile vanished from Alannah's face as well. "Okay. The short version goes like this: I am a tourist guide writer. My employer hires me to go to a given planet or station, see the sights, and write some helpful and engaging facts about the place. They pay for my expenses and work, and I go where they want me to."

Richard crossed his arms over his chest. "I think I can see where this is going."

"Yeah." Alannah cringed. "I'm not making excuses for myself. My employer said they wanted me to go with an expedition to this planet. To write up some articles and fact lists, so they are ready for publication as soon as... They said that with its proximity to Kaaloen, it won't be long before this world is included in the Union anyway. But..." She trailed off.

"Who exactly is your employer?" Richard asked. He was pretty sure he knew. Dietrich had mentioned a connection to Starlite Planetary Guides, one of the top three names in the interstellar tourism industry. But he wanted confirmation.

Alannah's mouth clamped shut. Then she shook her head. "Oh, whatever. I'm under an NDA, but at this point, I don't think I'll be much worse off for breaking it."

"Probably not," Richard agreed.

"Starlite Planetary Guides," Alannah sighed.

Eddie let out a low whistle. "The bigger they are," she said.

She was right. For them to sponsor one of their writers traveling to a restricted world... And not only their writer. They had endorsed the whole enterprise. A major lawsuit was waiting to happen here. Every human authority involved with interstellar relations would be lining up to have their heads.

"So you came here with a... hunting party?" Richard prompted.

"Yes. I didn't know that at the time, I swear!" Alannah added, an expression of pure agony crossing her face. Richard knew that whatever was coming next, it was going to be bad. "I thought they were here to do research. But... They are a team who take tourists here to hunt the most adorable native creatures. When I learned that was what they were really here for, I tried to talk some sense into them. I tried to stop them from going. But no one was having it and... Well, that's how I ended up cuffed to a chair. But you haven't told me anything about yourselves yet. Who are you? Are you here to save the animals?"

Richard and Eddie exchanged a look. So, this tourist guide writer was fine going to a restricted planet until someone wanted to shoot kittens or whatever equivalent thereof it had.

"If we can," Richard said. "We were hired to take the people who broke the planet's isolation into custody, and get them off this planet, leaving behind as little evidence as possible."

"That includes me, right?" Alannah said, her gaze flickering to Richard's gun and back to his face.

"Yes," he said because there was no use sugarcoating it. "But if you fully cooperate with us, that is likely to make a difference in your favor."

She nodded. "All right. As long as you promise to do everything you can to save the wildlife here, I'm all yours."

Richard Hart was not here to save the wildlife. Not specifically. But he supposed that was related to making sure humans got off this planet and did not leave any proof behind.

Turning the proposition over in his head, Richard couldn't see any way their new acquaintance would benefit from somehow double crossing them. Not unless she had a way to warn the hunters that they were coming and thus getting back into their good graces. But she was not planning on that. He was certain of that. Genuine regret radiated from her expression and body language.

"Sure," Richard said. "Let's track them down. The hunters become the hunted."

"Oh, you did not just say that," Eddie replied with another eye-roll. "Even you cannot be that cliché."

Richard wished for a reason to start barking orders just to stop Eddie's critique.

"So... Are you from the Terran Defense Force? Or did the draevere hire you?" Alannah asked.

"We are discreet, independent agents," Richard told her, smoothly avoiding telling her who hired them. "I'm a private investigator. Eddie is my pilot."

Alannah nodded. A smile, trying to conceal her insecurity, Richard thought, lit up her face. "So you are the human, interstellar version of Worra and Darith?"

"No," Richard said. He was not going to be compared to that piece of superficial wendek entertainment.

Eddie deliberately turned her face so Richard couldn't see what she said next.

"Okay, Worra," Alannah laughed.

"I beg to differ," Richard told them both. He thought he knew exactly what kind of remark his pilot had made. "Darith has more of your... qualities. But never mind that. Alannah, I need to know everything you know about the hunting party. How many they are, what they are armed with, who their leader is." He drummed his fingers on his thigh. "But we need to get out of the nest now, so you will have to brief us on the way."

Eddie elbowed him to get his attention. "I admit I was wrong," she said.

"About..?" Richard prompted, not wanting to assume.

"About not being able to find a tour guide for this dirtball," she said, grinning.

Sure, we are all Category 3 here, but before you leave the comfort of a human spaceship or station for a planetary destination—or even a ship or station tailored to the needs of another species—you will want to do a bit of research on what climate to expect.

You simply don't want to go to a tropical Dwebl paradise wearing insulated clothes better suited for the northern hemisphere of Wenamak. Or be surprised by the rainy season of the temperate zones on Ærou (unless you happen to bring diving equipment). In short, don't find yourself in them, shorts, that is, if you are headed into a blizzard.

Below, Starlite Planetary Guides has assembled a handy list of the climate and weather that you can expect of some of the most popular tourist locations. If your destination of choice is not on the list, rest assured; we have published separate guides for every thinkable planet and station in the galaxy!

- Alannah Jackson, *Interstellar Sightseeing 101*

11

ON THE PROWL

On a scale of discomfort from one to ten where one was relaxing on a beach in the shade of a fragrant tree with a delicious drink that was unfortunately not ice cold… And ten was huddling up next to a heating pipe in the slums on Yellowstone Station, broke, disowned by your family, and going without hyper for two weeks, Eddie would rate trudging through the winter landscape of Motarpria as a tentative five. It was not the suckiest place she and Richard had gone. It wasn't the most dangerous one, either. It was only cold. And boring.

Alannah's usefulness as a guide was limited. Obviously, the others hadn't told her exactly where they were going, so she could only give Richard and Eddie a general direction. She was no match for Richard when it came to tracking, either. But she kept up with their pace well.

"Do you do this a lot?" Eddie asked her when they took a short break on the bright slope of an iceberg or whatever. Eddie wasn't sure if mountains were considered icebergs when they looked like they were made of ice. She wasn't a geologist.

Richard was doing something with his patch. Eddie couldn't think of what that might be since a place like this had no PlaNet, and they were too far away from anything to get a connection to VoidNet. He could send her a direct message, but that was about it. She supposed he might be plotting in their progress on a rudimentary map. That was a very Richard thing to do.

Alannah wiped the back of her gloved hand across her lips after taking a sip of her canteen. "It depends on what you mean by 'this'," she said, thoughtfully. "Chasing the people who brought me to an illegal planet with two mysterious investigators? No. This is my first time. But wandering in the wilderness of a planet in general, yes, I do this a lot. It's part of my job."

"We aren't mysterious," Eddie said.

Alannah quirked an eyebrow. Her gaze flicked to Richard, still absorbed by his patch. Was he writing his memoirs or what? "You appear out of nowhere on a forbidden planet claiming you were sent to stop those poachers. You haven't told me who hired you or anything else."

"That's... classified," Eddie replied. "Anyway, I just take orders from him." Technically, that was true.

"Hm. That does qualify as mysterious in my book." Alannah pursed her lips, studying Richard for a moment before looking back at Eddie. "I would have assumed an investigator needed good hearing."

"What?"

Alannah smiled. She had a damn nice smile. "I didn't think you had a hearing impairment too. I'm just wondering."

"He isn't deaf," Eddie said. "He can hear us talking. Only, it makes no sense to him. Something about a virus that ate the bit of his brain that processes speech, I think. How did you know?"

Alannah's smile widened. "He clearly lipreads when he talks to us."

Eddie nodded. That was pretty observant. "I've always wondered if tourist guide writers really go to all the places they talk about, or if they just dig up some clips or whatever and write something based on other people's experiences," she changed the subject.

Alannah straightened her spine, and though she remained perfectly calm, Eddie knew she'd committed some kind of faux pas. "I can't speak for everyone," Alannah told her in a tone that matched their icy surroundings, "but the good ones always go to the places they write about."

"Right," Eddie said. And Alannah was, by her own definition, one of the good ones.

"Though we don't usually go to restricted worlds. That was so... so..." She made an angry gesture. "So stupid of me," she finished.

Eddie looked down and kicked at the snow. There was only a thin layer of it right here compared to the dunes they'd had to walk through several times already. Well, yes, it was pretty fucking stupid. But who was she to talk?

"All right," Richard said into the awkward silence. "Picnic's over. Let's get a move on." He stood up, rolled his shoulders and picked up his backpack.

"There's a distinct lack of sandwiches for this to qualify as a picnic," Eddie remarked. "And no alcohol."

"No drinking on the job," Richard said. "And the sandwiches would freeze."

"Yum. Sandwichicles." Eddie grimaced.

"You just *take orders* from him. Sure." Alannah muttered out of the corner of her mouth.

Eddie wasn't sure what that was supposed to mean, but decided not to ask. With someone else, she would have assumed it was a suggestion that she and Richard were romantically involved, but as she had just demonstrated, Alannah was really observant.

"How long do we have before starset?" Alannah asked.

Richard was watching her, a sarcastically raised eyebrow concealing his surprise. "I assumed you had an idea of Motarpria's day cycle?"

"Well, yes. It's 21.5 Earth hours," Alannah said, a sheepish expression stealing over her. "But my patch... um, ran out of battery a while back, so I don't have a watch." She held up her hand. "And... it takes a while to recharge this one."

Eddie was not super into new technology, unless it involved spaceships, but even she could tell Alannah's patch looked ridiculously outdated and battered. Her own patch never ran out of juice. But an old thing like that might take hours to recharge, she imagined. "Wow," she said. "Did you pry it off the wrist of a dinosaur?"

"It's fine for taking notes, and I had a state of the art camera retrofitted into it," Alannah said, slightly defensively. "I don't believe in discarding perfectly good gadgets just because they're a few years old."

"Okay," Eddie said. But Alannah probably just needed to take clips and stills of the places she went. More than she needed being able to play the latest games or connect to any net in no time.

"We have seven hours before it gets dark. Long summer days up here," Richard offered.

"Wonderful summer weather too. Wish I'd have brought a bathing suit," Eddie said, turning away from him.

"If you are done being sarcastic, let's get a move on," the uncrowned king of sarcasm said. He was too good at reading her even without, well, reading her. "I want to scale that slope and see if we can catch a glimpse of our quarries from a better vantage point."

The slope in question was more of a small mountain. Eddie considered mentioning that her salary did not include compensation for having to deal with nature, but she had been the one who insisted on coming along. She could have been sightseeing on Kaaloen or hanging out in a bar on Satarim Station right now instead of freezing off her nose and sweating buckets in her insulated underwear at the same time. It turned out that wading through the snow was a lot harder than it looked. It was worse than grav boots.

But Eddie appeared to be the only one who didn't enjoy this close encounter with the landscape. Richard was focused, sure, but he was so damn energetic. And Alannah...

"Oh, look!" the writer exclaimed and grabbed Eddie's arm. She was pointing at some snow-covered vegetation.

Eddie followed her gaze. A small, furry thing, almost indistinguishable from the landscape, was munching on something, holding it between its front paws. One set of legs was firmly planted on the ground while the last set was scraping in the snow. Eddie wondered if an extra set of limbs would make it harder to keep track of her feet or easier to keep a foothold. But then, piloting a ship was a bit like having extra limbs, especially when you were on hyper.

"I need a still. Damn," Alannah added. She looked up at Eddie with a pleading and slightly manic glint in her eyes. "Eddie, please?"

Eddie swiped at her patch to get to the camera function.

"Stop," Richard said.

They both looked at him.

"This planet is restricted, remember?" he continued. "You don't want evidence on your patch that you were here, Eddie. I have what we need on mine."

Alannah sighed. "Never mind," she said. "You scared it away, Richard. It's gone now." Thus saving Eddie from having to disappoint her. They continued to the crest of the slope-slash-mountain when Richard motioned for them to stay back. He lay down on his stomach and put on his visor. It would have made perfect sense if they were looking for an enemy army or something. But his soldier act felt a bit like overkill when they were looking for a total of 12 people who were both oblivious to their presence and probably pretty far away.

Alannah dropped to lie flat on the ground too and pushed herself up to Richard.

That left Eddie standing and feeling pretty awkward. Oh, to hell with it. Her clothes were supposed to be waterproof.

"Are we going to make snow zetois now?" she asked under her breath as she joined them on the ground. No one appeared to appreciate the joke. She put on her visor as well.

The heat signatures showed a few tiny creatures scattered around the landscape. Probably the family of that six-legged furball or something. But as Eddie moved her gaze up, she caught sight of movement further along. Way down and... She switched on her patch's distance calculator. Only a short walk. Zooming in, she smiled. Jackpot. Twelve little human-shaped heat signatures moving away from them.

"Got them," Richard said.

"I think I see them," Alannah said. She didn't have anything to enhance her vision, but when Eddie took off her visor again, she could still make out some incongruous shapes in the distance, now that she knew where to look.

Richard flipped up his visor too, stood up, and brushed snow off his clothes. He didn't even look like he felt silly for pulling that soldier move unnecessarily. Maybe he enjoyed flailing around in the snow. "All right. They aren't moving fast. We can catch up to them in another hour if we keep a quick pace. Eddie?"

Eddie made a mock salute. "Aye, aye, Captain," she said.

He nodded. "Alannah?"

Alannah blew out a breath. "Yes," she said. "I can keep up. I'm used to hiking."

I once read an old argument from pre-Union Earth. It went like this, "Guns don't kill people. People kill people." The argument was linked to an association advocating that everybody should be entitled to carry firearms for self-defense. Mind you, these were old-fashioned kinetic weapons they were talking about. They weren't called that back then. Just guns, rifles, pistols or revolvers. Because all firearms were kinetic, they relied on the ability to shoot a projectile that would enter another person's body and do great damage, often resulting in death.

The opposition, as we all know, eventually won out, limiting the possession of kinetic guns to authorized, trained law enforcement and military personnel. While this undoubtedly had something to do with guidelines already established in the Union, it is my belief that most humans supported it.

Since dart guns became a viable alternative, the use of kinetic firearms has been further restricted. It makes perfect sense in a galaxy where we all claim to respect the lives of others. Why would anyone choose a weapon designed to end lives when they could as easily opt for a dart gun loaded with projectiles that only temporarily paralyze or render the target unconscious? (And asking that question, we might as well wonder why lethal darts are even in existence today!) Even EMP guns, though quite brutal in some cases, surely are preferable to lumps of metal boring into flesh, bone, and organs.

This guide will take a closer look at the current members of the Category 3 species in the Union and their stances toward both military and civil use of weapons.

- Alannah Jackson, *Our Peaceful Galaxy?*

Ms Jackson,

As endearing as your personal observations usually are, this is going far beyond the acceptable scope for a travel guide. We need inspirational ideas for tourists—not a moral lecture, and even less so a loaded political one!

- Lisa Boucher, rejection letter to *Our Peaceful Galaxy?*

12
INTERFERENCE

Richard chose a vantage point to take a closer look at their quarries while everybody was catching their breath after the hike through Motarpria's perpetually white, untouched summer landscape. Well, untouched but for the group of humans in the valley below... and Richard, Eddie, and Alannah. The latter had spent much of the trek admiring the landscape. From the snow-covered hills and mountains generously strewn all over to the sparse, tall vegetation that Richard thought of as trees regardless of their lack of an actual trunk in the middle of them. Richard supposed that was an inherent trait of the trespassing writer. Eddie had mostly complained about various body parts freezing off despite the insulation she was wearing.

Through his visor, Richard studied the group before them. They all looked like giant marshmallows in their puffy, white clothes. Only the more sinister kinetic rifles they were carrying ruined the benevolent looks.

Richard counted the hunters once more. He looked back over his shoulder at Alannah. "How many did you say they were?" he asked, even if he had made a headcount at the last sighting too and knew he was coming up one short this time.

"Twelve," the writer replied.

"I was afraid of that," Richard muttered.

"What's wrong? Is 12 an unlucky number or something?" Eddie asked.

Richard returned his gaze to the group below once more. Using his visor to zoom in on them did not change the fact that there were only 11. "One of them is missing," he said, scanning the scene for any traces. Despite his elevated position, Richard could not see everything. And there were plenty of snow covered rocks and vegetation to hide a person if they moved away from the group.

Alannah said something.

Richard turned to her again.

"But where would they go? Why would they split up?" she asked.

"Maybe one of them is trying to find something to shoot," Eddie suggested, which was exactly what Richard was thinking. That or doubling back to attack them from behind... But he had already checked, and no one was sneaking up on the three of them.

The person who appeared to be in charge of the hunting party was handling his weapon with ease, raising it to eye level and pointing it away from the group. He lowered it again and turned to face the others, giving Richard a clear view of his face.

Richard snapped a couple of stills of the scene. Then he zoomed in on the man's face. "Their leader is making sure everybody understands how to not accidentally shoot each other," he summarized.

Eddie said something under her breath.

"No," Richard replied, venturing a qualified guess, as he turned to the others, "if they killed each other, we would have to drag their bodies off this planet. We want them alive."

"Fair," Eddie said, proving Richard's guess correct. "So what now?"

Alannah looked like she was trying to figure out if they were joking.

"Well, technically, we have what we need. Our contractor only needs confirmation of human activity here."

"But," Alannah said, "you are going to stop them too, right? That's what you said."

Richard nodded. "Yes. That is our secondary objective. We had confirmation the moment we saw their camp. And before that from their chick's traces in the atmosphere. We'll take them into custody."

"I hate to be a killjoy," Eddie said, "but there are 12 of them. Or 11 and one unaccounted for. Can we take them?"

"Yes," Richard said. "Most of them are only tourists. If we take the leaders, they'll fold. Do you agree with the assessment, Alannah?"

She blinked. "Um, I... think so. But... they have guns."

Richard patted the holster at his hip. The one in plain sight. "So do we."

"What happened to not wanting to drag bodies off the planet?" Alannah asked, her face as appalled as a wendek sniffing a wet dog.

Richard realized she didn't know what kind of darts were in his and Eddie's weapons. She might not even realize they were dart guns. He smiled at her as reassuringly as he could. He and Eddie were both armed with more than darts. She had her knife and a shocker on her, and he had a kinetic gun as well. "This is a dart gun. It's loaded with C class darts. The ones," he added for clarification, "that will knock out a human target for a short while."

"Oh," Alannah said. Relief spread on her face.

"So," Eddie said, rolling her shoulders, "Do you want to shoot the leader and see what happens, or should we play it safe and pick off a few of them?"

"Well, my plan is to—"

Alannah made an exclamation and pointed in the direction of their quarries, waving her finger up and down in terror.

Richard followed her gaze. And did a double take. A group of gigantic, six-legged animals were marching toward the group. The biggest of the animals had tawny, shaggy fur. The two smallest ones were almost completely white.

He looked back at the hunters. They had not spotted the flock yet. Foothills and rocks and glaciers were shielding the animals from view down there. Maybe it would be possible to—

Realizing an intense discussion was going on around him, Richard tore his gaze away from the scene.

"What the fuck?" Eddie exclaimed. "What are those? Weird, alien horses?"

"Horses don't have tusks. Or six legs," Alannah said.

"I know that! Hence *weird* and *alien*," Eddie retorted. "I may never have actually seen one up close, but I know what horses look like."

"The party is here to hunt them!" Alannah continued. "Look at the poor babies!"

"Good fucking luck to them," Eddie replied. "Those are huge!"

Before Alannah could continue in indignant outrage, Richard cut in, "With the kinetic guns they are carrying, they can easily take out the small ones. Maybe the big ones as well. Alannah, are those predators?"

"Yes, they are here to kill the innocent animals!" she shrieked.

"No, the animals," Richard said. "Are they likely to attack the hunters?"

"I prefer the term poachers," Alannah replied. And then, "I don't know. Can I borrow a visor?"

Eddie obediently handed over hers.

"Okay," Alannah said after a short silence. "I think they are harmless. Herbivores, probably."

"With enough feet and mass for them to trample us in seconds, and horns coming out of their mouths?" Eddie said.

"Tusks. Like Earth elephants. Woolly elephants," Alannah corrected her. "Probably for self-defense. If the placement of their eyes is anything to go by... like mammals on so many other planets, they are not predators. We have to save them! You said you'd save them!" She looked from Richard to Eddie, her eyes round and panicked, so much more than when they had surprised her in the tent.

"You didn't say they were the size of a small chick!" Eddie argued. "You said they were cute!"

"That is beside the point!"

Richard had made no promises. Well, he'd said he would stop the hunters, but he had no idea how to get the animals out of the way. Maybe if they could sneak up on the hunting party quickly enough to—

Alannah said something Richard didn't see. She tore off the visor, thrust it at Eddie, and whirled around.

"Where are you going?" Richard demanded.

Alannah yelled something as she began to run.

"How is that like urnoll? They don't even remotely look like urnoll! Are you crazy?" Eddie shouted after her. "She wants to scare the alien horses away from the hunters," she continued to Richard, though he had kind of guessed the gist of it. "Do writers not have any sense of reality?"

Richard shook his head. "She's not giving us any choice," he said. He imagined Alannah would try waving and shouting to scare the creatures away. She might even succeed if they weren't startled into trampling her. The problem was that the animals were not the only ones who would notice her antics. She might end up in the line of fire from the hunters' point of view. Someone might shoot at her accidentally. Or on purpose. And she would definitely blow any element of surprise on his and Eddie's part. All they could do now was to get within dart gun range of the hunters as fast as possible. "Come on," he added, pausing only long enough to get a confirmation.

"Yes, sir," Eddie said, snapping a mock salute at him.

Richard began to run. Despite her snark, Eddie followed orders and ran after him. Alannah, though... Alannah was an idealist. They were dangerous to a chain of command.

As they ran and skidded down the slope toward the hunters, Richard and Eddie saw Alannah veer off to intercept the animals plowing their way through the snow at a steady, slow pace.

Timing was everything. The snow turned into ice beneath Richard's feet, and he stretched out his arms for balance. He was surfing now rather than running, approaching the poachers at a breakneck speed. He had a brief vision of himself toppling over and rolling downhill, accumulating so much snow and ice that he turned into a giant snowball before ramming into the group. He gritted his teeth.

Eddie glided past him, saying something he could not possibly catch. She was carrying herself well, keeping her balance. She was a lot more graceful on her own feet than the stunt she had pulled landing the chick. Richard had a feeling she had done this before. Snowboarding. Or water skiing. Something like it, at least.

Ahead of them, the hunters were in disarray. One of them had spotted Richard and Eddie approaching and was alerting the others. Another had noticed something else. Richard chanced a quick glance to the side. Alannah was still bolting at full speed. And the small herd of not-quite woolly elephants was now in line of sight of every human on the planet.

The man Richard had pegged as the expedition leader was shouting at the others. As Richard tried to slow down, bracing for the possibility of having to throw himself on the ground, the man raised his kinetic gun and aimed it at Eddie.

"Twelve o-clock!" Richard roared at her back. "Get down!"

Eddie didn't hear him—No, wait. She bent her knees, somehow managing to crouch and stay on her feet. As the crack of the rifle rang out, Richard flung himself down and rolled, hoping for the best. He caught a glimpse of Eddie unbending before he found himself face-first in the snow.

Something hard struck him. Or rather, he struck it. But at least it stopped his mad topple. Richard did not allow himself to catch his breath before he got to his feet again, unholstering his dart gun. The world was spinning and lurching around him and melting snow was getting into his eyes. He blinked, tried to focus on his targets.

Ahead of him, voices blurred into a weird cacophony of noise as his vision began to clear. Eddie was down. Damn. Eddie was down! But, Richard realized as he brought up his gun, so was the man who had shot at them. Had Eddie rammed into him?

Indiscriminately, Richard aimed and shot two of the hunters in rapid succession. The darts went through their insulation almost unimpeded. "Drop your weapons and hold your hands where I can see them!" he roared. He almost announced himself as Terran Defense Force by sheer habit. "Drop your weapons!" he repeated, limping toward the group. "Eddie? Eddie!" he added, trying to keep the worry out of his voice.

Two of the hunters immediately tossed aside their guns. Then four more. Only one began to raise his. Richard fired another dart at him and watched him crumple into the knee-deep snow. "I will shoot all of you if I have to!" he shouted.

Everybody began to comply. Except the expedition leader who was staggering to his feet, gun still in his hand.

Richard's breath came out in a huff of relief as Eddie too got up. She was swaying, trying to steady herself, but she brought up her dart gun and pulled the trigger at point blank into the chest of the man in front of her.

He made a flailing motion, trying to backhand her, and then he sank to his knees and onto his side like the others.

Eddie turned to Richard, blood trickling from one of her nostrils. Her face was lit by a nearly maniacal grin that made Richard wonder if she had injected any hyper that he was unaware of. "I used to surf with my nephew and his dad on Wenamak as a teenager," she said by way of explanation, and then licked blood off her upper lip.

She was not seriously hurt. Richard shook his head at her. "Okay," he said to the group at large. "Everybody listen up! We are here to take you into custody on the charge of violations against—"

A loud bang cut off anything else Richard would have liked to say. A kinetic rifle shot, he was pretty sure. It was followed closely by a strange noise, not quite a squeal, not quite a roar, and not quite a whinny. But it was loud, too.

Eddie spun around, raising her weapon.

Dart guns were not going to be of any help here, though. The flock of animals were stampeding toward Richard, Eddie, and the hunters. And they would not be much impeded by running into everyone and trampling them.

"Move!" Richard shouted. "Everybody move, move, move! Help your companions get out of the way!"

A few of the tourists wailed and ran in a panic just like the stampeding beasts, with no regard for helping anyone else.

Richard took hold of the first unconscious person he could reach and wrapped his arms around her to pull her out of the animals' path.

Eddie was shouting at him. He looked up at her.

"...if Alannah was there!" she was yelling. "She might have been shot! Or trampled!"

"Eddie!" Richard interrupted her, "Get out of the way and take that guy you shot with you! Now!"

She was protesting, but he didn't have time to look at her. Alannah had made a choice, and he hoped she was all right, but none of them could do anything for her right now. Once things were under control, they would find her.

He was trying to track where everybody went. Most of the hunters were huddling together on the slope Richard and Eddie had descended. A few of them were carrying the third unconscious hunter between them. A single person was running in one of the only two wrong directions. Directly away from the animals, sure, but right in their path. Another was bolting to the other side, and Richard had a gnawing suspicion that they were trying to get away from him and Eddie as much as from the stampeding flock. Damn. What the hell did they expect to get out of that? There was nothing in that direction.

"Get the last one and guard them!" Richard shouted at Eddie who was looking extremely unhappy about the whole thing. "Take away their weapons and watch them closely!"

Eddie replied something.

"I need to catch the last idiot before they get too far away," he replied, unceremoniously dumping the unconscious woman in the snow by her companions, and then continuing to run.

The flock was already on top of where they had all just been. The rhythm of their feet, or hooves, or whatever, reverberated through the ground as they thundered on, each still making that earsplitting hooting noise. They blurred past him at breakneck speed, and Richard did not stop to look after them. He bolted across the trampled path of snow toward the hunter trying to get away from him.

I think most of us remember the stories about what happened when humanity settled on Johnson and how everyone had to scramble to minimize the damages to nature there.

When it comes to wildlife on foreign planets, my advice is simple. Treat nature like you would a protected national park or wildlife sanctuary on your home planet. If you are a station dweller or are unfamiliar with the guidelines, please allow me to sum up the essence:

Do not approach, touch, pick up, or otherwise engage with wild animals unless you have clear instructions that it is okay to do so. This is not only for your safety, but for theirs as well. Despite decontamination procedures, you might still be carrying something dangerous to animals. Or you might damage them in some way by touching.

As for plant life, approximately the same rules apply. Though you can approach most plants safely. (Vegetation is largely stationary, but there are exceptions.) In addition, however, it probably goes without saying that you should never eat anything in nature without confirmation that it is safe.

- Alannah Jackson, *Interstellar Sightseeing 101*

13
THE CATCH

Alannah ignored Richard and Eddie calling her. She tore down the slope, not in the direction of the poachers, but headed for the flock. It was a good thing she was used to hiking in all sorts of weather and climate... Though she hadn't ever run through snow like this. It did remind her of playing ball by the sea on Zhao. A lot colder, yes, but the snow wasn't unlike the deep and sticky sand on the beaches of that human settlement.

Now, however, there was a lot more at stake than not scoring a goal with a bright blue ball. The poor animals would walk into an ambush if she didn't do anything to stop them. She wasn't, she realized, entirely certain how she was going to achieve that goal. Probably, it would involve a lot of arm waving and shouting and hoping for the best.

The slope petered out, thankfully, and let Alannah slow down enough to catch her breath before either smashing right into the flank of one of the woolly cuties, or ending up sprawled right in front of them in the snow.

They really were huge. Even if she stretched, Alannah wouldn't be able to put her hand on the shoulder of most of them. "Don't judge anybody by their size," she told herself, which was very solid advice when dealing with species of varying statures. She just really hoped she was right about these creatures being herbivores.

She jogged as if her life depended on it and stopped short right in front of the flock. The woollies actually came to an abrupt halt before she even started flapping her arms. That was encouraging. They made a number of startled-sounding grunts, eyeing her warily.

"Hi," Alannah said, wondering if she ought not to look these creatures in the eye or refrain from smiling with her teeth showing in order to appear less threatening. Then again, she meant to turn them around. She spread her arms and bared her teeth. "I'm dangerous!" she yelled. "Shoo! Turn around!"

"What the hell are you doing?" another voice shouted.

Alannah had a weird moment of disconnect with reality. The woolly cuties were speaking to her? But no. That wasn't it. Another human was standing to the side and behind the flock. Someone with the dangerous end of a rifle pointing at the animals. The missing poacher.

Alannah had to get the flock moving. Now. "Waaaaaah!" she cried at the top of her voice, flapping her arms, running at the animals.

It almost worked. They even began to move. And they might have actually turned around and run back the way they came if not for the fact that the poacher's gun went off behind them with an earsplitting crack.

Alannah flinched. She dove for cover, throwing herself in the snow, rolling up in a tight ball with her hands locked behind her head with her arms protecting it. The flock was galloping, if that was the proper name of a gait that involved six legs, past her, a few of their hooves landing dangerously close to her. But thankfully, none of them hit her.

"Why are you not with the others?" the poacher was shouting.

Alannah finally dared to look up and then unfold herself, and climb to her feet again. The flock was running at breakneck speed toward the poachers. Alannah hoped Richard and Eddie had already intercepted and disarmed them. But she couldn't tell from here. She turned to the poacher she could see. The woman was taking long, purposeful strides in her direction. It was one of the expedition leaders, Jessica.

"I said, why—" The poacher stopped. "It's you!" she spat. "But we left you at the camp! How the hell..?"

"Tada. Surprise!" Alannah said in lack of anything more intelligent. She was a writer, dammit. Not a witty action hero.

Jessica aimed her rifle at Alannah.

Alannah swallowed. "Are you planning on shooting me?" she asked, her voice as even as she could make it, which wasn't very.

Jessica hesitated and looked nearly as uncomfortable as Alannah felt. She might be a poacher, but she was not a murderer of humans. Not yet, at least.

"That gun," Alannah continued, nodding at the barrel, "was made to fire a projectile powerful enough to take out an animal five or ten times my size. Do you know what's going to happen if you fire it at me? Brains and gore. All over the place." She might have swallowed a mouthful of snow earlier. It certainly felt like she had a fist-sized lump of ice in the pit of her stomach. She wasn't cool or calm, exactly. Just very much aware that she had to turn the situation around. And the only way to do that was to do what she did best. No, she was not an action hero. But as a writer, words were her weapon of choice. "Bone splinters and intestines," she continued. "Really messy. And if Ernest wanted to kill me, he would have done it already."

"The situation has changed!" Jessica said, not terribly convincingly.

"Yes, it has," Alannah agreed. "And if your boss wants me dead, he can leave me behind out here. But I suggest we ask him."

Jessica didn't lower the rifle. She was hiding behind the false security of it. And, rightfully, the rather real security. She was studying Alannah's face. Then her gaze slipped sideways and past Alannah, and her eyes widened. She took a step forward, finally lowering her weapon.

Alannah had no idea what the poacher was looking at. She hoped it wasn't a pile of dead woolly cuties. What she did know was that this was her moment of opportunity. She stepped in close, put a hand on Jessica's shoulder, and slid her foot in to kick away the poacher's feet out from under her.

Jessica yelped and did, indeed, fall.

Alannah took hold of the gun, making sure she was aiming the bad end of it away from herself. She wrenched it to the side, twisting Jessica's wrist and making her let go.

Yes! It worked. It actually worked in reality as well as in training. She had only ever done this to other people on a soft mat and with a fake gun. Alannah took a step back to watch the poacher get to her feet again.

"You little bitch!" Jessica hissed.

"Come on," Alannah said, ignoring the outburst. "I want you to meet my new friends. They should be right over there." She waved the gun in the direction the flock had gone. "Go on. Poachers before bitches."

And now she finally had the opportunity to look at the scene ahead. Yes, the woollies were long gone, the only sign of their flight trampled snow with big, bucket-sized hoof prints pockmarking the ground. And up ahead, a group of people sat huddled together, some of them slumping oddly against others. Only one was standing. Alannah's lips widened in a grin. Eddie. Eddie was keeping the group under control, her dart gun resting comfortably in her hand.

But where was Richard? Oh, there. He was heading for the group, more or less dragging another person. Someone must have tried to escape. Alannah did a quick head count and came up one poacher short. Again.

Richard spotted her and Jessica. His hand flew to the gun holster on his hip. Then he seemed to realize who was in charge and relaxed.

Alannah waved cheerfully at him. "Hello," she called.

"Who the hell are they?" Jessica asked.

"My new friends," Alannah said again, opting for letting Richard and Eddie decide how much they wanted to tell the poachers.

"Alannah!" Eddie cried out. "Are you okay?" She made sure Richard was close enough to watch the group before approaching Alannah and her catch.

"I'm fine," Alannah said. "And you?"

Eddie looked... Well, she looked a bit ruffled and had a scrape on her cheek and what looked like the remnants of blood crusting on her upper lip. But apart from that, she looked fine. "We rounded them up no problem," Eddie said with a nonchalant shrug. "That's the missing hunter?" She nodded at Jessica.

"Poacher, yes," Alannah said.

"You disarmed her?" Eddie asked, a little too surprised for Alannah's taste.

"Yes. Is that very hard to believe?" Sure, Jessica was taller than her, a lot of people were, but the poacher wasn't exactly a professional wrestler, or soldier, or anything.

"Um, I guess not?" Eddie shook her head. "You're just..."

Alannah scoffed. "I might be a bit of an idealist, but do you honestly think I would travel the galaxy alone without some kind of self defense training?" Maybe she hadn't had the opportunity to try it out very often. Or at all... But she had taken a course and practiced the moves when she could, and Jessica had gone down easily. "Anyway," she continued to Eddie, "Do you know how to turn this off?" She nodded at the heavy rifle.

Eddie blinked. "It's a kinetic rifle. You put the safety on..."

Alannah cautiously held out the weapon to her. The sooner that thing was out of her hands, the better.

Eddie took it, did something with the trigger and then something mechanical with, Alannah assumed, the safety.

Richard turned to them and motioned for Jessica to join the group on the ground. They all had cable ties around their wrists. Even the ones who looked half unconscious. "Good work," he said. And then, "If you worked for me, I would have words with your about taking off on your own like that."

Alannah smiled. "I had to do something. So... The woolly cuties got away safely?"

"Yes," Richard confirmed.

"And all the poachers..?" She let the question hang.

"Except one who ran." Richard made a gesture in the direction the animals had stampeded.

"Oh," Alannah said, scanning the group again. "That would be Niels. The pilot," she added.

"I have to go get him," Richard said, grimly.

"He could be far away by now," Eddie noted.

"I don't think so," Richard said with a grimace that Alannah couldn't quite decipher. "I think I caught a glimpse of him when I apprehended the other one. He looked very... stationary."

Alannah's stomach lurched.

"Do you need help?" Eddie asked.

"I need you to stay and keep an eye on the group," Richard said.

"Can I do something?" Alannah heard herself ask.

Richard studied her. "It might not be pretty."

"I know," she said, wondering why she was volunteering for this. Because she was a writer who, for the sake of her work, never backed out of a potentially unpleasant situation? But that usually only involved eating things that came out of, from her perspective, the wrong end of an animal. Or jumping off cliffs with only a thin rope between her and certain death. Or getting lost in a part of a settlement where no one spoke Standard very well...

Still, she had to do this. She had to make up for being so gullible. Face the consequences of going to Motarpria. So she set off, keeping pace with Richard once more. None of them spoke until they reached the lump in the snow.

Richard kneeled next to the unmoving man, carefully pulled down his collar enough to feel for his pulse. Then felt the back of his neck. The head moved like that of a creepy doll in a horror movie. "His neck was broken," Richard announced and looked up. To see her reaction, she assumed.

Alannah nodded. Swallowed. "Well, it could be worse," she said.

Richard's eyebrows rose. "He's dead. How much worse do things get in your world?"

"No, I—" Alannah stammered, "I didn't mean... Only that there could have been a lot of body parts where they shouldn't be. And there isn't. So..." She swallowed again, trying to find a way to make this sound a little better than it being about her personal relief that the dead man hadn't been torn apart. "Maybe it was quick?"

Richard nodded. "It probably was."

"Still, I—I didn't want them to kill the woollies, but I never wanted any of them to die, either. And," she added, reality slamming into her like a docking accident, "if we hadn't gone out here... If I hadn't gone the other way, I could have helped you get everyone to safety..."

"Alannah," Richard said, his voice firm, but not unkind. "Casualties happen. We did our best to limit them among the animals as well as the hunters with the means we had at our disposal. We accomplished our objective. Second-guessing isn't going to help anyone. Not you. And not him." He jerked his head toward the corpse, but he kept looking at her.

Alannah nodded. "Yeah," she said, not fully convinced.

Then Richard turned to the task ahead. He opened his backpack and pulled out a bag made of some kind of thin material that was roughly the size of a... Oh. Of a body.

"You are bringing him back? That's nice. It will give his family some closure," Alannah babbled.

Richard only looked back up at her in time to see the last part of this. "Well, we can't leave him. Imagine the dominant sentient species of Motarpria finding him."

A fair point. Still, Alannah didn't know if she ought to feel relieved or extremely disturbed that the man carried around a body bag. She decided to just help him straighten the dead poacher and arrange his limbs so he could easily be put into the bag.

When visiting another planet or space station, it is important to show respect and courtesy to the local population. This is true anywhere, but settlements and stations belonging to your own species will automatically seem more easily decipherable. The homes of other species might appear strange to you, but please remember they are exactly that: Someone's home.

Even if you have done extensive research, you are still likely to be surprised. I knew exactly what was going on, theoretically and from interstellar pop culture, but the first time I went diving with an åayu, it was still a startling and beautiful experience to see xem adapt to the environment so fully. Experiencing the galaxy first-hand is something else.

The customs and traditions, and perhaps even laws, of some species might appear odd to you, but imagine how your ways must seem to them. You would still want other species to follow your customs, right? Or at least respectfully try?

Finally, let's not forget that like humans, some of our fellow sentient neighbours, have culturally or ethnically specific settlements that may differ from even the norms of their other settlements. It's important to adapt and be thoughtful wherever you travel.

Don't let these differences deter you! We live in a wonderfully diverse galaxy. And there is always help to be found in Starlite's guides.

- Alannah Jackson, *Interstellar Sightseeing 101*

14
TEAM BUILDING

It was a real mood killer, Eddie thought, to be dragging a dead body along. Richard had decided to remove the cable strips from an alternating pair of the tourists so they could take turns to do the carrying. Eddie was glad she didn't have to. The decontaminating inner lining of the body bag kept the corpse fresh, as everyone knew from watching crime shows, but the literal dead weight was heavy. And not just physically.

At least the poachers were extremely cooperative. Shooting a few of them with dart guns and then saving their asses from a stampede had done wonders. That combined with the sobering experience of the pilot getting killed and Alannah's antics. She was pretty cool for a writer.

Richard took up the rear of their strange procession, keeping everyone covered with his gun, which probably also played a big part in the compliance of the hunters. He was carrying a couple of their kinetic rifles. So was Eddie. And Alannah, although Eddie had seen him disabling hers as well as the remaining few that were riding with the pilot's body.

"You okay?" Eddie asked Alannah, who was making up the front with her.

Alannah gave a short laugh, her breath coming out in a small cloud in the cold air.

"Yeah, I mean..." Eddie said. Alannah was right; it was a pretty stupid question.

"You mean apart from being asked by my employer to join an expedition to a restricted planet and discovering that it was an illegal poaching trip, being threatened with guns, almost trampled by the wildlife, and having a dead body in tow?" the writer summed it up.

"I guess," Eddie replied.

Alannah looked thoughtful for a moment, frowning and staring off into the distance. "I could be worse," she said at last. "My feet are dry and warm."

Eddie shot a glance at the aforementioned appendages in order not to meet their owner's eyes. "I'm not an expert on the legal stuff," she continued, "but you were pretty much in the dark about all this, right? You even tried to stop them. There shouldn't be any consequences for you." She looked back up at Alannah.

"Ignorance is bliss?" Alannah shook her head. "It will be their word against mine, but..."

"And ours!" Eddie said, a bit more heatedly than she meant to. "The authorities will listen to Richard."

Alannah looked back over her shoulder, past the row of poachers-turned-captives. Richard was striding along behind them as if this was all in a day's work for him. Okay, so it kind of was all in a day's work for him and Eddie. But not for Alannah, and Eddie found herself kind of wanting to protect their new... friend? Yes, she decided. Friend.

"Thank you," Alannah said. "I hope you are right. But Starlite knew what they were sending me out to do. They sponsored the trip. I will try to put a stop to something like this ever happening again, and I'll plead ignorance, sure... But even in the best case scenario, I'll lose my job."

"Right... But," Eddie added, "You're a great writer. You can get a new job, right?"

"You don't know I'm a great writer," Alannah said, not entirely unamused.

"The good ones go to the places they write about," Eddie paraphrased her line from earlier.

Alannah smiled. "Still, if word gets out I was involved in this... Even if it doesn't, I'll have to find a new publisher. It's a hard business to be in."

There wasn't really anything Eddie could say to that, so she didn't.

They were past the half-way mark of the trek back to the camp when snow started falling. Nice, fluffy snowflakes at first that made Alannah cup her hands to catch them and smile wistfully in a way that almost made Eddie want someone to smile at her like that.

But the snowfall grew denser, and the wind picked up. Behind her, Eddie could hear the hunters exchange worried remarks. She glanced at Alannah. "Is this going to be a problem?"

"I... don't know," Alannah said, biting her lip. "If it turns into a real blizzard, it could be a big problem. I'm sorry. There wasn't much data available on the weather here."

"Hm," Eddie agreed. Alannah had probably crammed the same information that she had skimmed before coming here. "Hold on." Eddie held up her hand. "Stop!" she ordered which, to her delight, everyone did. She jogged back to Richard to confer with him.

"Do we keep going or look for somewhere to wait this out?" she asked him. "Alannah thinks it can be pretty bad."

"It could take longer for us to seek shelter than just marching on," Richard said. A gust of wind and a wad of snow to his face made it painfully clear that the weather wasn't kidding about this. "But we need to make sure no one gets lost." He took off his backpack and started fishing out a length of rope with a grappling hook in one end. Had the man thought of everything for this trip?

Another blast of wind made Eddie stagger. One of the hunters actually did fall over and had a hell of a time getting back to his feet in the already deep snow.

"This is stupid," Eddie muttered. "It reminds me of this supposedly classic piece of literature I read in school where people kept getting caught up in dust storms, and it was clearly just a dumb plot device."

"Come again?" Richard asked, looking up at her and holding out one end of the rope.

"Never mind," she replied.

"Pull this through everyone's arms," he continued, not pursuing the matter. "We don't want anyone to get lost."

Eddie took the end of the cord that didn't have a grappling hook on it and got to work. Before she reached the front of the line and handed the rope to Alannah, she had repeated variations of, "Hold on to this," nearly a dozen times. From her perspective, it didn't really matter if they let go. Since their hands were tied in front of them, the rope would keep them in place regardless.

"Will this work?" Alannah asked.

"Sure," Eddie replied brightly. "It's like one big team building exercise."

Alannah's brows rose. "As if you ever enjoyed one of those," she said.

Eddie cleared her throat. She had, as a matter of fact, been forced to participate in several during her time in TWT. "What makes you say that?" she replied.

"You are not the type."

Eddie almost remarked that she didn't know it took a certain type, but then she remembered the bright-eyed, enthusiastic individuals who relished in teamwork. Eddie wasn't exactly anti-social, but as far as she was concerned, she was the one getting everybody through hyperspace in one piece, and everybody else was an interchangeable accessory to spaceflight.

Drawing an urnoll blindfolded while some cargo worker told her where to put the pen wasn't going to save anyone from colliding with a stray planetoid or being torn off course by hyperwind.

"We're good to go," Eddie told Richard through her patch. He usually had his set to audio to text, and she was pretty sure he wouldn't be able to see what she was saying in this weather. "Let's go!" she shouted to everybody else. She put on her visor to shield her eyes and began to walk.

The blizzard was getting stronger still, wind howling and snowflakes either turning into hail or just feeling like it because of the gale. Even with her visor and its useful overlays, it was stupid hard to stay on track. She hoped no one in general, and Richard in particular, noticed when she accidentally strayed in the wrong direction and had to circle back on the right track.

All things considered, it could be much worse. Only twice did someone fall over and yank on everyone else uncomfortably. So it really—

Eddie stopped abruptly. Alannah bumped into her back with a yelp of surprise.

"Shh!" Eddie hissed and squinted.

"What?" Alannah whispered in her ear, her hot breath tickling the small hairs on the back of Eddie's neck.

Eddie didn't reply. She resolutely ignored the accordion of people ramming into each other behind them, wanting to shout at them, but not daring. Something was out there. Something... alive. Something not quite big enough to be one of the woolly cuties—damn, now Alannah had made her think of them like that too.

"Status!" The word began to flash on her patch. It would take a moron not to notice something was going on, but Richard had the sense to send his message instead of shouting.

"I don't know," she whispered into the patch's microphone, not taking her eyes off the space ahead of them. "Something moved. Less than 50 meters ahead." She slid her dart gun out of its holster.

"What are you doing?" Alannah hissed.

In a whisper, Eddie repeated the message she had sent to Richard.

Richard who, Eddie discovered, was trotting up to them now as silently as a prowling syraxh.

Eddie pointed out the direction in which she had seen movement, and Richard's dart gun found its way into his hand as well.

"What is going on?" someone asked behind them.

Richard caught Eddie's eyes and made a chopping motion across his throat with his fingers.

Eddie nodded. She was going to interpret that as an order to keep the hunters quiet rather than decapitating them. She was also not going to voice that joke.

By silent agreement, Richard left Alannah in front of the group and asked Eddie to go through the ranks and keep everybody quiet. Eddie would have preferred a different distribution, but Richard was the boss, and Alannah might not have the authority needed to keep the others under control.

"Stay calm and shut up," Eddie stage-whispered to the hunters, keeping her dart gun in sight to casually suggest that if they didn't follow her orders, she would not hesitate to make them very quiet very quickly.

"Are we under attack?" the guy who was in charge of the expedition asked when she reached him.

"Maybe," Eddie replied.

"Then give us back our weapons!" he growled under his breath.

"Oh dear," Eddie hissed, "you still seem to be a bit confused from the last time I shot you."

He closed his mouth again and glowered at her.

Eddie wondered if Richard had found the thing she had glimpsed yet. It might have run away. Probably had, in fact. They should just—

Something moved in the periphery of Eddie's vision, somewhere in the dense whiteness. Eddie squinted. It felt like looking for a shadow moving inside a dark room. Feeling like someone was looking back at you...

All of a sudden, the shadow was right in front of her. Eddie instinctively brought up her gun. The creature wasn't nearly as big as the grown woollies, but still towered over her. Its short fur was whitish yellow, and it had six limbs like all animals they had encountered on Motarpria. But unlike them, this one was only standing on four of them. The front pair was more like arms than legs. The creature's head sat on a long, flexible neck that bent at an odd angle to stare at Eddie with small, fiercely yellow eyes. Its face had most of the parts Eddie personally felt should go in a face, but it had one too many mouths compared to practically any animal she had seen before.

Except... Animal may not be the correct term here unless you included sentient species in that category too. The creature glanced at the dart gun and back at Eddie's face. And there was something in the gaze that reminded her of the many species she normally mingled with on space stations and Cat 3 planets.

Both of the creature's mouths moved, and a string of sounds erupted from them. It sounded like speech. Sentences strung together with perfect syntax.

Eddie couldn't help thinking that this might be how Richard felt whenever someone spoke. She also, absurdly, wondered if it would make it easier or harder to speak while eating if you had an extra mouth. "Sorry, buddy, but I can't understand you," she said, and tried for a bright smile.

The creature drew back as if startled, then reached back with one arm and retrieved a long object from a sheath that Eddie hadn't noticed before. Was that a spear?

From somewhere behind the creature, Richard's voice rang out, "Everybody down! Now!"

Eddie did not think twice. When Richard Hart told her to get down, she didn't even ask how low. Just threw herself on the ground. She hoped everybody else did too.

The creature moved around, way too close for comfort. Close enough to see that they were wearing some kind of shoes.

After a couple of extremely long minutes, they turned and began to walk away.

New feet appeared in Eddie's line of sight. This time it was only one pair, and they were wearing familiar boots.

"You can get up now," Richard shouted.

Eddie got back to her feet. Behind her, everybody else was doing the same.

"What the hell just happened?" Eddie asked.

"They circled around you. I followed them," Richard summed it up. "You probably offended them because it looked like they were going to attack. I thought playing dead might do the trick."

"What's going on?" Alannah asked as she came up to them.

The hunting party was grumbling and complaining.

"Shut the fuck up!" Eddie yelled at them and then turned back to Richard. "I wasn't offensive! And how did you know they wouldn't attack anyway? That wasn't an animal! There's no way they thought we all just keeled over and died."

"I thought that showing them we were not a threat might help. I didn't want to interfere any more than necessary," Richard explained.

"Good," Alannah said, very loudly so that the hunting party was sure to hear her too, "because that would be disrespectful and potentially dangerous when you don't know the physiology of the species you are dealing with! Anyway, what did they look like?"

Eddie described the creature.

"That's a rahtiere," Alannah said.

"A what now?" Eddie asked.

"Rahtiere. The dominant sentient inhabitants of this planet," Alannah explained. "Or that's what the draevere call them. Didn't you read up on Motarpria?"

"Well, yes," Eddie said defensively. "But I kind of skipped that part. We were going to avoid them."

Alannah's expression was covertly judgmental and overtly flabbergasted.

"Which we did!" Eddie continued. "It's not our fault they didn't avoid us."

"I wish I could have gotten a still of you with them," Alannah sighed.

"We are not supposed to be here, remember? It's bad enough that they encountered us at all," Richard said as he started toward the hunting party, effectively ending the conversation by turning his back on Eddie and Alannah. "Come on!" he told the group, "Let's get out of here!"

"Okay, people," Richard called out when they reached the hunters' campsite. Thankfully, the blizzard was dying down now. "It's time to leave this place. But first, you need to pick up your trash."

"What are you, a park ranger?" one of them snorted. Eddie wasn't sure who.

Richard scanned the crowd, but he could not possibly have made out what the man said, so Eddie took over. "He's the guy giving you orders, jerkface," she said, "so you better listen and do what he says. Pick up your shit, you shit."

Richard cleared his throat. "I expect this place to look pristine when you're done," he said. "If not, it will be on the entirety of humanity's head, so get rid of your litter. I guarantee you won't enjoy the alternative." He crossed his arms over his chest, and the group began to disperse to take down the tent, and basically get rid of any evidence that humans were ever on this planet.

"Not you," Eddie said when Alannah began to move.

Alannah held up her hands. "Yes, me. I'm part of this. I need to make any amends that I can."

Eddie watched her approach the others. She earned a lot of scowls and sneers on the way. Eddie would personally kick someone's knee or crotch if they turned into more than that. Yeah, sure, Alannah had fucked up big time, but she was not like the rest of them. She hadn't come here to kill anything or disturb the natural order of the planet. She just wanted to observe and write. She didn't deserve what was coming to the rest of them, whatever that might be.

"We need to sort out the logistics," Richard said, as he stood beside her watching the unwilling cleaning team disassembling their shelter.

"Yeah," Eddie agreed. She knew what he meant. Once the place was spotless, they had to get themselves and the hunting party off the planet. And they had to take both chicks, obviously.

"We need to split up so one of us can keep an eye on them. But they are also one pilot short. I don't know if one of the others can fly, but..." Richard trailed off. "Can you make it back to our chick alone?"

"No. Or," Eddie corrected herself, "Of course I can, but I know what you're getting at and I am not letting you fly the small dick compensation chick. You fly like my grandmother."

"I didn't know your grandmother had a pilot license," Richard said, dryly.

"Whatever. Point is, you will bang up the *Colibri* trying to fit that into the nest or not be able to get beyond the atmosphere of this rock, or whatever. You aren't used to flying anything bigger than a shoebox," Eddie argued. "You go back to our chick and I take this lot back to the *Colibri*."

Richard's face did something complicated. "I don't like it. What if they try to overpower you? Force you to fly somewhere else?"

"They might do that to you as well, you know."

He changed his posture in a way that suggested he would be able to deal with a bit of a mutiny. Which was a load of bullshit. His military background would give him an edge in a physical struggle, sure, but there were 11 of them, and how was he even supposed to keep an eye on them and fly at the same time? Eddie could fly with her eyes closed and her hands tied behind her back. Practically. She tapped her lips with her forefinger. Got an idea. "Oy, Alannah!" she called.

Alannah looked up from the tarpaulin she was rolling up.

Eddie gestured for her to join them in the spectators' stand.

"I see where this is going," Richard sighed. "When did you decide to trust her?"

"When she tackled that hunter," Eddie said. Or maybe before. She really wasn't sure. But her gut feeling told her they could trust the writer. And her gut feeling was never wrong. Well, except for that one time...

"Yes?" Alannah asked.

"Can you fly a chick?" Eddie asked.

"No..." Alannah replied slowly.

"Can you use a gun?" Eddie continued, though judging from the way she had handled the kinetic rifle, Eddie thought she knew the answer already.

"Eddie," Richard cautioned.

She waved a hand at him dismissively. She knew she was overriding his authority, but she was pretty sure about this.

Alannah's gaze flicked to the weapons Eddie and Richard were sporting. "I... can't imagine a dart gun can be difficult at close range. I know which end the dart comes out of," she said. "Why?"

Eddie flashed Richard a smile. "Do you have a better idea? The hunters will be tied up anyway. How much trouble can they make?" she asked.

He made a sound that was almost a groan. "Fine," he said. "Alannah, we need you to go with Eddie while she takes those guys and their chick back to our ship. Specifically, we need you to make sure they don't try anything."

Alannah blinked. "But I'm one of them," she said.

"No, you're not," Eddie said.

"Yes, you are," Richard said at the exact same time.

Eddie glared at him.

"But," he added a little louder, "you are not like them. And helping us out now will count in your favor when we hand you all over to the authorities."

"Fair enough," Alannah said. "I'll help you. If they complain, can I be really authoritative with them?"

"Sure," Eddie said.

"I don't want any violence," Richard said, though Eddie had a hard time picturing Alannah resorting to violence just for the hell of it. "Get them to the ship safely, okay?"

"Sir, yes, sir," Eddie said in the least military way she could possibly muster.

"Of course," Alannah replied, then jerked her head in the direction of the hunters. "I'll go back and help make this place spotless. But, um... Thank you. For trusting me. No matter what happens after all this, I really appreciate it. And the chance to thwart those people."

You might have heard of the internet, the world wide web, the cloud, or cyberspace. Those are all terms that describe the digital world of pre-Union Earth. Before humanity settled on other worlds or had any meaningful relationship to other sentient, technologically advanced species, communication was confined to our home world. The structure, using artificial satellites and towers as relays, probably seems familiar to you because that is largely how our PlaNet works. PlaNet is the invisible infrastructure that our patches and other devices access in order to let us send messages, watch the news, and so on. Despite the name, a PlaNet does extend to include any space station in orbit.

But PlaNets are still local. If we want to reach spaceships, other worlds or stations further away, we access VoidNet. Generally speaking, VoidNet consists of what interstellar travelers bring with them. Every ship is equipped with a device that automatically picks up and deposits large quantities of data when in the vicinity of so-called *buoys* distributed not only near human stations and settlements, but also in other species' space. It is a very efficient method that was established by the Union a long time before humans even knew it existed.

Of course, the transfer through buoys is not exactly instant. So if a message is extremely urgent, it is possible to use a courier service made up of Apodiformes (and Strigiformes, although they don't usually cater to civilians) class spaceships whose sole purpose it is to bring digital data back and forth. This, however, can be quite expensive.

- Alannah Jackson, *The Interstellar Pony Express*

15
A JOB, WELL, DONE

Eddie, Alannah, and the hunting party made it back to the *Colibri* well before Richard. After he edged the chick in beside the larger model, Eddie entered the nest and assessed his parking which was, thank you very much, perfectly fine under the circumstances.

"How did it go?" he asked her.

"Without a hitch," Eddie replied. She had already changed back into her usual snug-fitting clothes and did indeed look perfectly at ease. "Well, almost."

"Almost?" Richard echoed.

"Well, that expedition leader called Alannah a double-crossing bitch and a few other rude and misogynist things," she replied. "But only after we got back to the ship. So I had my hands free."

"To..?" Richard prompted despite himself.

"Punch him in the mouth. I think Alannah could have done it, but she's too polite. And someone needed to."

Richard wasn't convinced that was the case, but there wasn't really anything to do about it now. "I told you I didn't want any violence," he said. "Where are they now?"

"We locked them up in the two unused cabins."

"Did you... feed them?" Richard asked. He didn't personally care, but it was a matter of being professional. A matter of treating prisoners right... Strange. They had never had any prisoners on board before. Unless you counted that syraxh a client had accidentally left behind on a station a few months back that they had to chase down and bring back to her.

"Yeah. Alannah said to. She's very into being proper," Eddie added.

"Good," Richard said and wagged a finger at her. "You could learn something from her."

Eddie only grinned as they made their way through the ship.

Richard unzipped the outer layer of his clothes. It was much too warm on the *Colibri* for this. He raised his arm and checked his patch. It was late, from his and Eddie's subjective point of view.

"Do you want to stay in orbit here?" she asked, possibly reading his mind.

"No," he said. "Not if you can fly safely. I'd rather not have any draever surveillance noticing us."

Eddie snorted. "Of course I can fly safely. I used to do 20 hour shifts in the pilot's seat."

"Yes. On hyper," Richard returned dryly.

Eddie glared at him, but she didn't argue. "I can fly," she said.

"All right, then get us to Satarim Station. We'll dock there and get some sleep before making the jump back to Stonehenge..." He trailed off. The *Colibri* was small. They weren't in the passenger or freight business. Sure, they had a bit of extra space, but Eddie had put the detainees in the two spare cabins. That was crammed enough as it was. Putting them all in one would hardly be possible, and he would rather not risk having them anywhere else on his ship. The nest was bigger, but they would also be able to do a lot of damage from there. Medbay was out too. The body of their pilot was stored there, and...

"Richard?"

"Alannah," he said. "Where do we put her up?"

"I was thinking the empty storage unit across from the galley," Eddie said.

Richard shook his head. "No. That's not fit for human habitation."

"I'm kidding," Eddie said, rolling her eyes. "Alannah can sleep in my cabin."

"All right," Richard agreed. "Stack a couple of inflatable mattresses for her. Your bunk won't fit two people."

"Well, that depends," Eddie said with a smirk. It was entirely ruined by the rapid succession of a sheepish smile that Richard could not help wondering about. "Okay!" she continued briskly. "I'll head to the cockpit!"

When they finally emerged from hyperspace into the Hawking system the following subjective day, Richard could not wait to get the mob of unwilling passengers off his ship. As soon as they were in PlaNet range, he sent a message to Colonel Micah Dietrich to let them know the *Colibri* was approaching with the desired cargo on board.

The hunters had known better than to make too much obvious trouble, but by the time Richard took off from the *Colibri* in the ship's chick, he had dealt with an accidentally, quote unquote, blocked toilet, a faked medical emergency, and a real case of claustrophobic panic. And a quietly fretting writer, despite Richard's reassurances that he would put in a good word for her. Granted, she had made a mistake, but she didn't deserve having her career snatched away from her.

Richard went directly from the chick to his client's offices where he met the same lieutenant as the previous time.

"Ah, Captain Hart, sir," the lieutenant said, covering his bases in terms of etiquette. "Colonel Dietrich is expecting you." He touched the display on his desk.

Dietrich's voice, presumably, emerged from a speaker.

"Captain Hart is here to see you, Colonel," the lieutenant said.

Another short string of words from the speaker

"Yes, Colonel." The lieutenant touched the display again and looked back up at Richard. "They say you can go in now," he reported earnestly.

Richard couldn't help smiling. Quick learner. "Thank you, Lieutenant," he said and crossed the distance to the door of the inner office. It slid open to admit him.

Colonel Dietrich was seated at their desk, reading something. They looked up as Richard entered, and the display between the rods disappeared. "Ah, Captain Hart," they said. "Please sit down."

Again, Richard resisted the urge to salute. Despite everything, his body automatically wanted to snap to attention when dealing with a superior officer. With what would have been a superior officer if he had still been in the Force, he reminded himself. "Thank you, Colonel," he said and sank into the offered chair across from Dietrich.

"Tea?" the Colonel asked. They had already poured a steaming cup for themself, and the pot was sitting on the desk next to an empty cup.

"Please," Richard said.

Colonel Dietrich picked up the teapot and poured the thin liquid into Richard's cup. They replaced it and looked up at him again. "We can talk," they said, meaning, Richard assumed, that the office wasn't under surveillance, rather than the two of them actually sharing the physical ability to formulate words. "Thank you for your message, Captain Hart," they continued. "I will send my people to your ship to take the perpetrators off your hands as soon as we are done here."

"Thank you," Richard said. "We apprehended a party of 12 poachers. Or 11... Unfortunately, one of the perpetrators lost his life."

"Due to..?" Dietrich prompted.

Stupidity. Richard managed to bite off that answer before it reached his lips. "An accident. He was trampled by local wildlife."

"I see." The Colonel tapped the side of their cup with an index finger. "I would like your verbal account of the whole mission."

"Yes..." Richard took a sip of the hot tea. He really would have preferred black brew. He cleared his throat and began a chronological, detailed account of his and Eddie's adventures, beginning with the draever Liyaa and ending with the return to the *Colibri*. He described the nature of the hunting trip and how Alannah had been involved. For a moment, he considered not mentioning her at all. But even if he let her off the *Colibri* without any incident, the hunters would surely mention her during their trial. And Starlite would too. So Richard was honest about all of it. He had never been a great fan of writing reports, and delivering the account verbally was nicely refreshing.

Dietrich did not interrupt him. They also did not take any notes. Richard had half expected them to pull out a sheet of paper and start scribbling with their antiquated fountain pen. But they did not even ask for the stills stored on Richard's patch. Just leaned in to look at them, making Richard feel like a teenager sharing something secret.

"Are you going to need an official statement from me?" Richard asked at the end of his tale.

Dietrich's eyes narrowed in thought. "No," they said slowly. "The perpetrators' chick will have enough data on board for us to prove its flight to Motarpria. That is enough to warrant an aletheia assisted interrogation to get to the bottom of the matter if need be. And I should prefer to continue keeping our cooperation as discreet as possible. I may want to call upon your services again in the future."

"By all means," Richard said. He had to admit this was one of the more interesting assignments of his relatively short career as a private investigator. You could only uncover so many extra-marital affairs before it got a bit old.

Colonel Dietrich gave him a short smile. "As for the matter of payment..."

"Colonel," Richard all but interrupted them. "I... have a request."

Judging from the expression on their face, Dietrich was not used to anyone interrupting them. "Yes?" they said.

"The writer. Alannah Jackson. I took a look at her public profile. She appears to be a competent journalist, and I couldn't find anything on VoidNet suggesting she has previously had any brushes with illegal affairs."

"Yes?" Dietrich said again.

"Like I said, she proved very helpful to my pilot and me. And there is no doubt she was kept in the dark about the true nature of the expedition."

"Interstellar rules and regulations apply to everybody," Dietrich said dryly, "regardless of how sorry they claim to be after breaking them."

"I know," Richard conceded. "But... Perhaps the repercussions might be less severe if she pleads ignorance?"

"Captain Hart," the Colonel said, "Are you asking me to pull some strings to get her out of trouble?" Their voice was level and almost stern, but their eyes had an absolutely delighted gleam to them. It made Richard want to squirm in his seat.

"Not in so many words," Richard backpedaled. "But..."

"All right. I will look into her records. Including files that you might not have access to," Dietrich said. "I won't make her transgression disappear, but I might be able to... put in a good word for her if you are right about her qualities."

Richard smiled. "Thank you, Colonel." He had done his own investigation, but someone in Dietrich's position would have the security clearance to access more information than what was publicly available. Especially if Alannah had ever run afoul of any laws before. He wondered what the Colonel would find. He hoped it would not be anything bad. For Alannah's sake, but also, although he had not brought it up with her or even Eddie yet, his own.

"My pleasure," Colonel Dietrich said with a flourish of one hand and a quirked eyebrow that suggested they had somehow already figured out Richard's own vested interest. "Now, if there is nothing else we need to discuss," they added, "we should take care of your payment. Does the final tally of expenses match your initial estimate?"

"Nearly," Richard replied. He gave an account, also verbally, of the differences.

"Very well," Dietrich said. "I will arrange for a transfer. It will appear in your account as payment from my planning and maintenance department for the Terran Defense Force Intelligence. Effectively, you are a janitor as far as matters of bookkeeping are concerned. Which," they added at Richard's not quite successful attempt at suppressing a snort, "is accurate enough. Cleanup and maintenance of human-draever relations are essential."

"Yes, Colonel," Richard said, swallowing his grin. He had never been involved in the budgeting aspects of the military, but he knew that wasn't what maintenance usually meant.

"In case anyone significant ever asks, you did some biological waste cleanup and basic ship repairs for us in the Kaaloen system. Should they press you further, you may refer them to me, and I will take care of it."

Take care of it... Richard's gaze flickered to the cabinet behind the Colonel's desk that most likely contained their personal arsenal of weapons. But no. There might be rumors of Dietrich's efficiency in the field, but Richard was sure that the phrase didn't contain anything as sinister as all that. As the head of military security on Stonehenge, the Colonel was a far too public figure for something like that now, and besides, these were, supposedly, their own people they were talking about.

"Understood," he said. "Thank you for employing *Colibri* Investigations."

The Colonel pursed their lips. "I have to ask. Why *Colibri*?"

"It's a small bird," Richard explained. "Good at prying into things and being discreet about it."

"I see."

"And it's the name of my ship," Richard added.

"But she's a—" Dietrich cocked their head ever so slightly, which made them look a bit like a confused kitten. But then they shook their head, deciding not to pursue the matter. "Very well, Captain," they said instead and stood up.

Richard followed suit. He was usually good a reading a room. Good at observing and finding the subtext. And right now, he had the feeling that Dietrich's comment about using his services in the future was based in intent rather than in politeness. He couldn't help wondering if he had just become an irregular of the Terran Defense Force's Intelligence Department. And if so, exactly how that made him feel.

"Thank you for your services. It has been a pleasure to do business with you."

Richard took the hand the Colonel offered. "Likewise, Colonel Dietrich," he said.

"To travel is to live" is a quote usually ascribed to one of Earth's old storytellers. Allegedly, he said this back in the nineteenth century, hundreds of years before humanity took off from the planet to explore space. Even before we launched any ships to the local Moon or put artificial satellites into orbit. The journeys of that time were, therefore, restricted to the continents of our home planet. But crossing an ocean or even traveling by the ancient railways from one location to another could easily take longer than any trip from one solar system to the next today.

Whether the storyteller was being strictly literal is a good question. After all, he was a writer, so in a sense, he provided readers with another mode of travel. There are many ways of experiencing the world, or worlds, and dreaming can be traveling too.

The destination is usually important when you plan a trip. But so is the journey. Traversing the galaxy is not only the void between destinations. It is the ships and the sights you take in while in transit. And it is the people you meet and the friends you make along the way. Leaving familiarities behind, whether you embark on a business trip, a holiday, a research expedition, or something entirely different, traveling will give you more than just the new experiences and sets of stills and clips on your patch. It will also give you a new perspective. It might even teach you something unexpected and set you on a new and better course in life.

On that note, I will leave you to start exploring the galaxy on your own. Safe travels!

- Alannah Jackson, *Interstellar Sightseeing 101*

16
A NOT-SO-CLEAN SLATE

Alannah supposed she'd been let off the hook comparatively easily. There had been a few interviews with the authorities. There had been talks with lawyers. Richard and Eddie stayed on Stonehenge for the first part of the exhausting proceedings, but they had not testified due to some secrecy regarding their employer.

During Alannah's private meeting with the attorney assigned to defend Starlite Planetary Guides, the lawyer had suddenly looked up from her display and frowned at Alannah. She had tapped her fingers thoughtfully on the table at which they sat for a long moment until Alannah, trying not to sound too scared, eventually asked if something was the matter.

"No," the lawyer had said, slowly, "Nothing you need to worry about. On the contrary, in fact." When pressed, she had expanded this into a vague explanation that she had received a report supporting Alannah's innocence and moral character from a reliable authority, and that this would greatly help her case. She wouldn't go into more detail, which felt entirely unfair. Alannah wondered if her mysterious benefactor was Richard. She couldn't imagine who else it could be.

At the end of a grueling string of days that felt like months, there had been a trial, but for Alannah's part, that had gone down without incident. She testified against Starlite Planetary Guides and their associates who had arranged the trip to Motarpria. If looks could kill, Alannah had a feeling she would have keeled over lifeless, twice. First from the glare she received from Lisa Boucher, and then from the one directed across the courtroom from the expedition leader.

But unlike Starlite and Ernest and Jessica, Alannah sailed right through the proceedings with only a few verbal warnings, an ugly mark in her records and a fine. A mighty fine fine, indeed, but it was nothing compared to the ramifications that hit the entirety of Starlite. Whether there would even be a publisher of that name after all of this, Alannah wasn't certain.

It hadn't felt exactly right to plead her own complete innocence and ignorance, but in a way, Alannah had been ignorant. Or gullible. Or naive, definitely, which amounted to much the same thing in this case. She had truly believed the expedition was going to a planet that would be open to the public in a matter of months, or a couple of years at the most. She'd gone assuming they had a special research permit. But she had not insisted on seeing said permit. And she had not bothered to do her own research properly. Which was perhaps the most ridiculous and embarrassing thing about the whole affair from her point of view because research was what she did. She could kick herself for it. She already had shouted at herself in the mirror. Loudly. More than once. But that did not have the power to change the past, so here she was, still in possession of her freedom, but obviously without a job and utterly broke save for a very small amount of units in an emergency account.

Alannah left the courtroom relieved and happy and at the same time so upset she wanted to cry. The pipeline was one of the few luxuries she could afford now because it was free to the public. But she decided to walk for a while. She needed to clear her head. She needed to start planning what to do next.

Her feet took her first to the largest park on Stonehenge. Most stations with permanent human residents had areas like this because the early days of space travel had shown humanity that it needed a bit of nature now and again, even if it was lit by a small, artificial star set in the ceiling of the park area and controlled by automatic systems.

The park reminded her painfully of traveling to real planets, which was the point of the artificial landscape, but not the point Alannah needed. So she fled the premises, almost bumping into a Terran Defense Force soldier coming the other way. The soldier asked her if she was okay, to which she almost started laughing hysterically. It was only the soldier's long hair and very pretty face that surprised her enough to stay sober, and mutter her thanks before hurriedly continuing her flight.

She opted for the nearby space observation lounge as her temporary sanctuary. Ignoring the cluster of tourists in one end of the lounge, Alannah went to stand close to the viewscreen pretending to be a giant window to space. Naturally, it was an illusion because there was solid radiation-proof pelso plating between her and the void outside. Illusion. Void. Words that described her career and current mood pretty well, too.

Alannah breathed out through clenched teeth. A Diomedeidae class freighter passed outside, silent, looming, and faraway. She wondered if the *Colibri* had already left. She would have liked to say goodbye to Richard and Eddie. Would have liked to thank them again.

"Planning your next move?"

Alannah almost jumped. She wheeled around to see Richard Hart standing behind her. He must have crept up on her while she was lost in thought.

"I suppose," Alannah said, unconvinced and thoroughly unconvincingly.

Richard nodded and looked at the screen for a moment. His gaze tracked the same colossus of a spaceship that she had been absently staring at.

Alannah waited politely for him to look back at her. "Thank you. For helping me out. With the case and... everything," she said when she had his attention again. She couldn't help looking for signs that he understood this as a reference to the mysterious report the attorney had received. But if he did, he hid it well.

Richard smiled. "We all make mistakes," he said. "I've made a fair deal of them in my time. Eddie too."

Alannah shrugged, too defeated by her own mistakes to be curious about theirs.

"So what will it be? Your next move?"

She sighed. "I... don't know, really. I love writing, but I'm not sure any publisher would want me after all this. Unless I change my name and appearance, they will know I worked for Starlite..."

"Do you need a publisher? I thought everybody could publish what they want in this day and age," Richard wondered out loud.

"True," Alannah agreed, "but it's not as easy as all that. You need marketing. You need editors. And if you want to earn your keep writing travel guides, you need someone to sponsor your trips. I can barely afford a ticket off this station at this point. But I'll figure something out," she added. She always did. It wasn't the end of the world.

Richard followed another ship with his gaze, a military vessel this time, then turned to Alannah again. Talking to him always felt so intense, she thought, because he had to stare at your face all the time. "I want to offer you a job."

"What?" she almost spluttered.

"I want to offer you a job," Richard repeated.

"But... doing what?" she asked, the hysterical laughter she had suppressed earlier threatening to bubble to the surface again.

"Eddie and I can't keep up with everything. We can't be experts on every single planet we go to. We can't know every relevant cultural custom of every single species we meet. I'd like you to do the research for us and provide us with a second opinion from time to time. I can't offer you a handsome salary, but I can offer you a cabin on the *Colibri* and an opportunity to travel so you can write your guides if you want to."

Alannah wanted to throw her arms around the man and squeeze him until his head popped off. Or just short of that. This offer was almost too good to be true.

"As for the fine print," he went on, "it's not entirely risk-free to travel with us. We do deal with dangerous criminals from time to time, and we are very unpopular in some circles. We also," he added as an afterthought, "come with our various bad habits and drive each other nuts sometimes, and you'd be part of that. But Eddie likes you, and I'm sure you'd be a valuable asset."

"I... don't know what to say. Thank you," Alannah said, her heart fluttering.

Richard waved this away. "If you do accept my offer, I also need to stress that you will be under my command." He grimaced as if reverting to such military terms was an accident that physically hurt him. "What I mean to say," he resumed, "is that you cannot pull any stunts like the one on Motarpria. I obviously don't expect to bring you along for field work, but I need to make it clear that if for some reason I give you a direct order, you need to follow it without question or hesitation."

Alannah would have balked at this if not for three simple facts. One, she still felt a sharp stab of guilt when she thought of the pilot who had been trampled, possibly because she had bolted to divert the woollies. Two, it was not likely that such a situation would ever arise again. She was just going to do research. And three, she was more broke than she had ever been, and this was a job offer. A very, very good job offer.

"Think about it," Richard continued. "We leave the station at 20:00 hours local time tonight. I'll send you our location and a draft of the contract I can offer you. Show up if you're interested. If not, we'll leave it at that."

The thought that he was only doing this out of pity snaked into Alannah's mind. And then the idea that he might think he could get away with paying her next to nothing because she was in such a pickle slithered in after it. But... No. Richard Hart struck her as too honest for that sort of thing. And she was usually right about people. Unless, she thought, it involved poachers. Besides, did his motivation even matter that much right now?

"I have a room on Johnson," Alannah said. "I travel a lot, but there are some items I need if I'm going to stay on the *Colibri* for a longer period of time."

He nodded, calculating, it seemed. "We can swing by there and pick up your belongings, but I won't pay you until after that. Think about it," he repeated.

Alannah rubbed her temples. She thought about it. For around 20 seconds. "Let me see that contract," she then said, knowing that she would agree to it, almost no matter what it said.

Richard flashed her a grin and brought up his patch. "I'll send it right over."

Alannah hoped her outdated patch wouldn't die on her again before she managed to read and sign the contract. After a tiny delay, a ping told her there was a new message from a Richard Hart. A smile spread on her face. It felt like her first real smile in days. It felt good. It felt like a new beginning.

Acknowledgements

If *The Stellar Snow Job* were a movie or a TV show, you'd find the end credits right here. This is, in other words, where I get to thank a bunch of awesome people who made the book a reality.

So, first of all, I am grateful to Spaceboy Books in general for offering me a cabin on their amazing spaceship and sticking with me not only through my first trilogy, but letting me continue to explore strange, new worlds with *Colibri Investigations*. Thank you to Nate Ragolia in particular for perfectly polishing off my prose and being a hundred times better at coming up with catchy titles than I am.

My gratitude also to my wonderfully supportive family and friends who always have my back, and let me rant about people living in the future/my mind.

Very special thanks to my team of beta and sensitivity readers for providing me with invaluable feedback, asking the right questions, and loving my characters. Also thank you to the Fish Climbing Trees community and gratitude to my Patreon supporters Gabe Clark, Kosomolski, Ryan Watt, Skjalm, ZombiEdward, Nicole Fuschetti, and more. Your support means a lot to me!

Naturally, no acknowledgments are complete without my sincerest love and scritches to the resident cats who keep me company and purr everything better (and occasionally nap on my keyboard or block my view of the screen, but that's part of their charm).

And thank you! I hope you've enjoyed the first *Colibri Investigations* novella, and that you want to join the crew for another adventure soon.

Alannah stood in front of Eddie and Richard in the *Colibri*'s small galley. Her patch was projecting an image of their next destination on the wall behind her. "Dwebl," she announced, "is the zetois' first planet of settlement, so it dates back hundreds of Earth years before we even heard of the Union. Richard, you said your target is in Naiwon?"

Richard nodded affirmation. "That's as far as we could get with the insurance company's intel and our own qualified guesswork."

Alannah zoomed in on a sprawling city. "As you can see, Naiwon is adjacent to Dwebl's primary shuttle port."

"Shuttle?" Eddie echoed.

"That's the term zetois use instead of chick," Alannah replied. "Please remember that. It would feel odd to us if other species referred to our vessels as human babies."

Eddie snorted. "Right."

Richard cleared his throat. "Our target is probably trying to lie low. Alannah, do you know if there are any human neighborhoods or slums where he might hide?"

Eddie leaned back in her seat as Alannah began to summarize her research. One of the best things about having her on the team was how Eddie could concentrate on her own job and not have to do the homework.

About the Author

Marie Howalt was born and raised in the North European kingdom known as Denmark and decided to become a writer at the age of 11 when the local library's unimpressive supply of science fiction and fantasy ran dry.

Having graduated with a master's degree in religion and English studies with a primary focus on speculative literature, Marie wrote as a hobby and worked as a teacher and a translator between English and Danish for a few years before changing lanes in life due to the chronic illness PCS (Post Concussion Syndrome).

Fast-forward to the present, and you will find Marie writing as much as physically possible. The tales are longer and more complex than the childhood fantasies, but they still take place in the far future or alternate realities.

When not writing (or bribing imaginary people to tell their stories), Marie is dedicated to being a cat perch, but also voice acts, dabbles in videos, draws, and reads a lot of books. Sometimes, you can find Marie pushing art supplies and fancy fountain pens in one of Copenhagen's oldest shops.

Marie's first traditionally published book came out in 2019, and since then, there has been a steady flow of a book per year (plus the odd short story). *The Stellar Snow Job* is the first *Colibri Investigations* book, but the next ones are already in the works, so you won't have to wait for too long to join the crew again.

If you want to be kept in the loop, please drop by Marie's Instagram profile @mhowalt or www.mhowalt.dk, or support Marie's writing while getting special perks and previews at www.patreon.com/mariehowalt

Other Works by Marie Howalt

The Moonless Trilogy
We Lost the Sky (2019)
Seeking Shelter (2020)
Heart of the Storm (2021)

A Moonless Novelette
Training Wheels (2021)

About the Publishing Team

Nate Ragolia was labeled as "weird" early in elementary school, and it stuck. He's a lifelong lover of science fiction, and a nerd/geek. In 2015 his first book, *There You Feel Free,* was published by 1888's Black Hill Press. He's also the author of *The Retroactivist,* published by Spaceboy Books. He founded and edits BONED, an online literary magazine, has created webcomics, and writes whenever he's not playing video games or petting dogs.

Shaunn Grulkowski has been compared to Warren Ellis and Phillip K. Dick and was once described as what a baby conceived by Kurt Vonnegut and Margaret Atwood would turn out to be. He's at least the fifth best Slavic-Latino-American sci-fi writer in the Baltimore metro area. Shaunn is the author of *Retcontinuum,* and the editor of *A Stalled Ox* and *The Goldfish,* among others.

www.ingramcontent.com/pod-product-compliance
Lightning Source LLC
Chambersburg PA
CBHW030640190726
48286CB00008B/2602